Doc's Deputy

Arrowtown Book 4

By Lisa Oliver

Doc's Deputy (Arrowtown Series #4)

Cover Design by Lisa Oliver

Model and background purchased from Shutterstock.com

First Edition July 2018

Dedication

To all my lovely readers who've helped see me through a difficult month – please, never underestimate the power of the posts and comments you make designed to make me smile, drool on occasion, and remind me I am thought about. That means more than words.

To Pat, Amanda and Sue Ann – thank you for polishing my work

To Phil – Keep writing.

Table of Contents

Chapter One

Doctor Nathan Farriday, known as "Doc" by every Arrowtown resident, pasted a professional smile on his face as he ushered Mrs. Dash and her daughter out of the treatment room. The smile was more for Rosie, the sweet little fawn who was forever having trouble controlling her wee legs. Mrs. Dash, like most of the other adults in town, was well used to his grumpy ways.

"No climbing, running, or lifting anything heavy for at least a week and no getting that cast wet," he warned as he led them to the front door.

"We know the drill by now." Mrs. Dash managed a tired smile of her own. "Come along, Rosie. We'll get that ice cream I promised you for being so good for the Doc." She leaned towards Doc and whispered, "I half think she gets into so many scrapes, just so she can have ice cream."

Doc thought it was more likely Rosie was trying to emulate her six older brothers who thought their baby sister was a nuisance, but it wasn't his place to say so. His smile lasted until the door closed behind them then his shoulders sagged, and he let out a long sigh. Flicking off the lights, he locked the door and made his way upstairs to his open plan apartment.

Shrugging off his shirt, Doc scratched absently at the gray leather skin coating his stomach as he bent down to see what was in the fridge. Mrs. Hooper from the store had already been over and stocked his shelves. She was worth every cent he paid for their little arrangement. Doc had long since lost the urge to cook for himself. He pulled out a large container – lamb stew by the smell of it. Doc's stomach rumbled appreciatively. Mrs. Hooper had a tongue like an acid bath and an attitude to match, but she was a damn fine cook.

Five minutes on a slow heat in the microwave and Doc's dinner was ready. He sat at his two-person dining table, watching out the window at the night life of the town. Not that there was much to see at seven in the evening. The library and the main shops were closed, although Cam's bar was already doing a steady trade. Open seven nights a week, the place was always busy. His heart jumped as he saw a bike peel away from the sheriff's parking lot, but it quickly slowed again. He recognized the bike. It was Liam, on his way home to his mates and baby. Rocky, the new sheriff, and Mal, his sidekick, were already at Cam's. Doc could see their bikes parked outside. Doc sighed. Rocky was prone to getting into trouble when he drank, although he'd been a lot more responsible since he'd been voted into the Sheriff's job.

That means Deputy Joe is working alone tonight. Doc hated that he knew that. He hated the quickening rush of blood to his dick and the worry that flooded his mind. For all his sneers at the boy in person, Doc was confident Joe could look after himself. A cousin of the last police chief, who'd been run out of town due to his corrupt actions, the deputy was a buffalo shifter and built like the young bull he was. The problem was the boy was just too nice, too decent, *and too fucking young for the likes of you.*

Annoyed with the way his thoughts were running away from him, Doc hurried through his meal, washing the single bowl in the empty sink before turning off his lights. To the outside world, it would look as though he'd gone to bed early – although, as the only doctor in a fifty-mile radius, no one would hesitate to knock on his door if he was needed. Using the benefit of his shifter-enhanced sight, Doc crept back down stairs to the basement.

Shoving his pants down his thighs, Doc kicked them off and let his shift flow over him. Shifting was something he never dared to do in front of others. His kind were venomous to anything walking on two legs or four. Although, the snake shifter Simon seemed to cope with living with others and shifting among them – even with his little mouse mate, Darwin. But Doc never dared take the risk. He'd only ever shifted once in front of another person. He shuddered when he thought of the result.

Do no harm, he reminded himself. *It's* why he became a doctor after all. *Don't think about deputy Joe. Don't think...don't think...don't....*

/~/~/~/~/

Joe sighed as he looked at the clock on the wall, while slamming the filing cabinet drawer shut. 7:25 pm. It was the quiet part of his shift. The time when most good folks were enjoying meals with their families and curling up for an evening of watching television or going for a run in their shifted form. The trouble makers weren't usually around yet, probably drinking in a car or disused barn somewhere, getting up the courage to do something stupid. That's when he'd get called out, but that wouldn't happen until a lot later in the night.

Looking around the office, Joe tried to find something else to do. He could divert the phone and go home, but he didn't have anything to do there either. Usually at this time, he'd be patrolling the streets. Joe always got a feeling of pride as he wandered around the streets at night. Arrowtown wasn't a big town. It had everything a body would need. Many of the shifter families that lived there were second and third generation and Joe knew most of them by their first name.

But lately that pride had been dimmed and tinged with guilt. Since talking to Liam a month before, Joe was more conscious than ever that his mate – his unclaimed mate – lived just down the road. Oh, he'd known about Doc for ages and who they were to each other. He'd been shy at the time, hopeful that the man would approach him. His cheeks flamed as he recalled the one time he'd broached the topic of their mating with the grumpy older shifter.

"Young, dumb, and well hung. Three things I don't need in my life. Now, get the hell out of here and never speak to me again unless it's in your professional capacity."

Fuck. Joe rubbed his chest. Those words still hurt, months later, and it wasn't the sort of sentiment he could just shrug off and ignore, like he could when he got similar comments from his family when he was younger. He considered himself an honorable man. He would not push himself where he wasn't wanted, and Doc had made his sentiments very clear.

Which led to his current predicament. Prior to his chat with Liam, and lord knows why he confided in the young lion of all people, he used to patrol the streets, keeping a close eye on the Doc's house. But now the words "he's my mate" were out there – had actually been spoken to another person, the pain he felt at being separate from the sexy older man increased. What was worse, he now felt like a pervert for all the times he'd kept the Doc and his house under surveillance. It felt wrong to do it now, even though his animal demanded no less, and in fact wanted a whole lot more.

"Damn it, fuck it all to hell!" Joe grabbed the night stick laying on his desk and threw it across the room, lodging it into the wall. "Oh, fucking brilliant," he announced to the empty room. "Now Rocky's going to take the cost of repairing that hole from my wages."

Striding over, he pulled his night stick from where it was sticking out from the wall and rubbed his hand over the hole. It was noticeable. There was nothing he could do about that. *Although,* he thought as an idea came to mind. *I've got some plaster at home. It's going to be a different color than the wall, but a patch job is better than the hole.*

Pleased he had something to do, even if it meant getting teased by Rocky and Mal in the morning, Joe grabbed his keys, diverted the office phone to his cellphone and headed out the door. It was only a twenty-minute walk from the precinct to his home, but Joe took the patrol car. If he got called out, he didn't want to get hell from Rocky for being late to an incident, on top of the damage he'd caused. It was definitely preferable to shifting. Joe didn't dare shift; hadn't done in months. His animal half thought his horns and solid head would make a useful battering ram against the Doc's door.

The drive was quick, and Joe was back at the Sheriff's Office before anyone noticed he'd gone. Stuffing paper into the hole, to give the plaster something to stick to, Joe was mixing the plaster into a smooth consistency when his phone rang. Cursing, because the plaster was the type to harden quickly, Joe put on his professional tone as he answered the call. "Arrowtown Sheriff's Office, Deputy Joe speaking."

"Joe, thank goodness I caught you." It was Mal, and he sounded rushed. "Are you still in the office?"

Joe looked at the paper stuffed hole in the wall. "Yep."

"Get over to old man Forest's place on the edge of town. He claims he's got a buffalo terrorizing his sheep."

"Shifter?" Joe was already moving.

"Has to be. No natural buffalo would chase down sheep. There isn't...you are...." Mal trailed off.

"I'm the only buffalo shifter currently allowed to live in Arrowtown if that's what you're asking. But you know that sheriff Quincy had a big family and none of them took too kindly to being kicked out or losing everything they owned."

"Damn it. I should have known something like this would happen." Mal sighed. "I'll drag Rocky out of here and we'll back you up, but…."

"Bring guns," Joe said shortly as he got in the car and turned the key. "You know darn well this is a trap to pull us out there. No shifter in his right mind would tamper with natural sheep. If I can't run this guy off, then there's no way two wolves can, even a mad-house like Rocky. Bring guns and be prepared to use them. I'm on my way."

Shutting off the phone, because he really didn't need any further details, Joe pushed the cruiser at full speed, his lights flashing. There was no need for sirens. There was barely any traffic, but his lights would warn shifted animals to get off the road. Rabbits were the worst, loving to play chicken with cars. Joe didn't mind most of the time, but they knew if the lights were going he wasn't going to stop and they'd better get out of the way.

Two minutes out from the Forest farm, Joe saw two individual headlights coming up behind him fast. Mal and Rocky were on their bikes, offering back up as Mal had promised. Part of Joe wished they hadn't arrived as fast. He hated shifting in front of other people after being teased constantly as a teenager about the size of his cock. *You're here to do the job you're paid for,* he reminded himself firmly as he swung his vehicle into the Forest driveway. Parking, he stepped out of the car as Mal and Rocky pulled up.

Old man Forest, no one had a clue what his first name was, was standing on his porch in a pair of white long johns that had seen better days and an unbuttoned red checkered shirt. Joe's eyes narrowed at the rifle he held in his hand. Forest was a wolf shifter – a lone wolf who kept to himself most of the time. He took a lot of ribbing from town members for running sheep on his land, but he barely spoke to anyone except Mrs. Hooper.

"That four-footed lump is up there in the back paddocks." Forest waved his rifle towards the back of the house. "I shot over his thick head and he charged me. He fucking charged me. I want him taken in."

"Mr. Forest." Rocky put on an alpha voice Joe had never heard before. "I can understand you're upset, but if you let me and my men handle this…."

"Handle it how?" Forest stumped down the porch. "Don't go waving your alpha mojo under my nose, boy. I was tackling alphas like you when you were still in diapers. If a wolf could've done the job, I wouldn't have had to call you. Two of my best sheep are caught in the fences. They don't deserve this shit."

"Deputy Joe is going to do his best to run the shifter off, Mr. Forest," Mal said smoothly as Rocky growled.

"Him? He's still wet behind the ears from when his mama washed him." Forest spat on the gravel.

"Mr. Forest," Joe seethed. "I'm getting really tired of people still treating me like a calf. I've been a deputy for five years and I know how to do my job. Now, are you going to stand there and bleat all day or let me do what you called us in for."

Rocky burst out laughing, slapping his thigh. "Don't look at me like that," he said when Mal glared at him. "It was funny. Wolf, sheep, bleat." Rocky cracked up again.

Wondering just how many beers his boss had had, Joe headed around the house on his own. It was fully dark, with only a sliver of moon inching its way up the night sky. But even so, the terrified bleating of the sheep in the top paddock and the looming mass standing in front of them were easy to see. Noting the two fences between him and the buffalo, Joe strode up the hill, not taking his eyes off the shifter. Climbing over one fence, he walked until he reached the second.

"It's a lot easier to talk if you shift," he said, not bothering to yell. The shifter could hear him easily enough and the sheep were traumatized enough as it was.

All he got was a stamping foot and a swinging head from the shifter. *Damn it, gonna have to do this the hard way.* He couldn't shift on his side of the fence, or he'd wreck the fence getting through it. There was also a risk of getting caught up in the wires, much like the sheep Forest was complaining about. But shifting on the same side of the fence as the buffalo also came with its share of risks. Joe would be vulnerable in the time it took him to morph into his animal side.

Realizing he didn't have a choice, Joe climbed the second fence, jumping down lightly on the other side. The buffalo was watching warily, snorting heavily. "You've got no right terrorizing old man Forest's sheep this way. If you've got a grudge against someone in the sheriff's department, then man up and come and talk to us. This is just bullshit and you know it."

The buffalo bellowed. Joe lifted his head and sniffed the air. *Fucking Sheriff Quincy. I should've fucking known.* Flicking open the top two buttons of his shirt, Joe quickly dragged it over his head. "As a duly deputized officer of the law, I'm ordering you to shift and surrender yourself."

Yeah. Like that was going to work. Quincy didn't take kindly to orders even when he was sheriff. The shifter lowered his head and pawed the ground. Joe couldn't work out what the old man wanted. He was banished from Arrowtown for life. Forest wasn't one of those who benefitted from the sale of his goods. Forest had nothing to do with any of the trouble in town…but…. It came to Joe in a flash. Old man Forest was the only *sole* land owner around for miles.

The perfect place for a fight. Fuck, this is personal. I should have known he'd come after me sooner or later. Joe was the only man currently on the force who'd worked for Quincy while he was sheriff. He was the only one found not guilty of corruption and the only buffalo who hadn't had to forfeit his goods. "Don't say I didn't warn you, Uncle Robert. You of all people should know I'll do my job whether you like it or not." Joe kicked off his boots. "As a banished person I have every right to take you in. You're trespassing."

The buffalo snorted and charged as Joe shoved his pants down his legs.

His buffalo answered the call quick enough, but Joe had barely shifted before his uncle came crashing after him. Dragging his pants that were caught on his back hoof behind him, Joe whirled around and lowered his head. Buffalo fights were all about strength, not speed. During the rut season in the wild, two male bulls would clash their heads, pushing against each other, trying to get the other to yield. At just over three thousand pounds in his shifted form, Joe was a third larger than the largest of his natural counterparts, but his uncle was a shifter too and not much smaller than Joe.

This is going to hurt. Joe had barely fought in his shifted form. When he was young, he and his cousins used to mock fight and as Joe slowly pulled away from his family, some of those fights got more intense. But that'd been years before. Joe's only hope was his uncle was no more capable of fighting than he was.

Horns clashed as they came together. Joe dug in with his hooves, using all the strength in his shoulders to push against the older animal. Instinct took over. They might not be fighting for the right to mate, but Quincy was threatening the town he cared about. The old man had taken bribes, ran the department into the ground, and cared little for anything except his power base. Now that was gone, and the older Quincy was frantic to get it back. Joe would've told him he was wasting his time if he could find the breath to do it. Fueled by his rage, the banished shifter was immensely strong.

Again, and again, they clashed. Joe managed to gain some ground, seeking to trap his uncle with the fence, but time and time again he got pushed back. As he twisted away, his uncle's lowered horn seared his flank. Joe's legs almost buckled under the pain. But pain could be his friend. He'd lived with it long enough and Joe was already angry. Oh, his anger wasn't directed at his uncle, but to his animal half it didn't matter. Any target would do.

Conscious of the blood pouring out of his side, Joe lunged and pushed hard. His uncle was caught off guard, probably mentally celebrating his win. Powering with his back legs, Joe drove his uncle into the fence causing the older buffalo to become tangled in the loose wires. He became aware of Mal and Rocky yelling at each other. Mal wanting to shoot and Rocky swearing he didn't know which animal to point the gun at.

"Use your fucking nose," Mal yelled.

"All I can smell is sheep shit," Rocky complained. Joe willed the man to stay away, but Rocky wasn't blessed with commonsense. Strangely enough, that same quality made him an excellent sheriff, but the last thing Joe wanted to see was Rocky's wolf form creeping closer. And yet, there he was, sniffing closer, his teeth bared.

Smelling his chance, Quincy pushed his head through the fence, one of the wires digging into his neck, but he was too enraged to notice. His horns were swinging wildly in Rocky's direction and Joe saw red. A buffalo's horns weren't overly long like an antelope's, but Quincy's curved outward and if Rocky got caught by one it would do a lot of damage. Backing up a couple of steps, Joe lowered his nose until it was brushing the grass and lunged for Quincy's underbelly. As his horns met fur Joe wrenched his head up, toppling his uncle onto his side, the fence crumbling underneath his bulk. The smell of blood filled the air and this time it wasn't Joe's. Thrashing his head back and forth, his uncle tried to get up, but Joe must have hit a major artery because in less than a minute, the older buffalo stopped moving.

Stumbling back, his chest heaving, Joe tried to catch his breath. Blood ran down his horns, churning his stomach and the gash in his side burned. "Joe?" Mal was approaching slowly, his hands spread to show he wasn't carrying. "You have an amazing shifted form, but you've been hurt. You need to shift so we can get you to the Doc."

Fuck no. The last thing Joe needed was to face his mate's disapproving glare. Pulling on the last of his strength, he shifted, collapsing on the cold grass. "I'll be fine," he panted. "It's just a scratch. Need to free the trapped sheep."

"Forest has already done it." Mal held out his shirt and pants. "They're covered in mud, I'm afraid. Shall I get a blanket from the cruiser?"

"I'll be fine." Pulling on his pants, which were ripped beyond repair, Joe was glad to see they covered his bits at least. He was in no mood for Rocky's brand of humor. "You'll be needed to help Rocky with my uncle."

"So, it was the ex-sheriff Quincy, I thought I recognized the stench." Mal grimaced. "Huh. There's nothing left to deal with. See for yourself."

Glancing over to the fence, Joe saw Quincy had shifted, his corpulent form still caught up in the fence wires. His unseeing eyes and the way his tongue lolled out of his mouth told Joe all he needed to know. "It wasn't intentional," he muttered as a wave of nausea hit him. "He went for Rocky…."

Mal's hand landed on his shoulder and Joe hid his flinch. "You did what any other man would've done. Quincy had no right to be here and he deliberately created a nuisance, so we'd be called in. I hate to ask this, but is there any chance this was a personal attack on you?"

"If he was going for you, he'd have used his gun." Joe swayed and put his hand out to stop himself from falling. "Can you give me an hour? I need to get home, clean up and get some food down me. Shifting has taken it out of me. I'll be back in the office in an hour."

"Take the rest of the night off. Liam's already covering for you." Mal leaned down and whispered. "Between you and me, I think he was grateful to be called in. Their little one is teething, and he's got lungs like a banshee."

Joe stretched his lips in the facsimile of a grin. At least he hoped that's what his face muscles were doing. "Thank him for me. I'll come in tomorrow to do the paperwork. Oh shit. I've got the cruiser. I'll...."

"You'll take it home and stop worrying about it. We can do without it for one night," Mal said firmly. "This is not your friend talking now, but your boss. Get your ass home and if those ribs aren't any better in the morning, you're going to the Doc and I don't want to hear any macho objections."

Joe knew when he was beat. He had no intentions of going to see the Doc, but home was a damn good idea. Staggering to his feet, Joe managed to hold himself upright long enough to walk past Rocky and Forest who were arguing about who was responsible for the cost of the smashed fence. Forest did stop haranguing Rocky long enough to call out, "you did good, young 'un. I didn't think you had it in you, but good job."

Lifting his hand in reply, Joe kept on heading down the hill. Every breath was a struggle and he knew he was on the verge of a breakdown. It was sheer force of will that stopped him collapsing. A force of will that lasted until he opened the door of his own home. Slamming it behind him, Joe fell on the floor, his teeth clenched against the pain in his side and the heavy ache in his heart. Quincy was his first, and Fates willing, his only kill. Shuddering, Joe curled around his wounded torso and let his tears fall. *There's no way my mate will want me now. I'm a murderer.*

Chapter Two

Doc scowled as he pushed his way through the crowd hanging around Hooper's store door. He wasn't in the best of moods, and he refused to consider it had anything to do with not seeing any sign of Deputy Joe around town in the past three days. And no, he wasn't going to ask after him. He had important mail to post and Mrs. Hooper's store was the only place in town he could do it. But it didn't stop him asking the woman in question why so many people were gossiping around her front door.

"Guess you don't hear much, holed up in that office of yours." Mrs. Hooper took the envelopes Doc handed over, pulling out her large book of stamps. "Word around town is our young deputy has finally found his fighting spirit. Took out his uncle on old man Forest's farm not three nights ago. Killed him in his shifted form."

"Young Liam has an uncle? What was he doing at Forest's place?" Doc felt a pang of concern. Liam was a new father and although he had two mates to help him through, Liam's temperament didn't lend itself to killing anybody.

"Not Liam, you silly old codger. Deputy Joe." Doc felt the blood fall from his face and he clutched the edge of the counter. Mrs. Hooper went on regardless. "Huge clash of the titans, if you hear Forest tell it, and he was there. Blood everywhere, young Joe injured. Forest felt for sure he was losing but then that piece of shit Quincy tried to gore Rocky, who was in wolf form at the time, and Joe pulled on some strength from somewhere. Ripped a hole in the old man's chest he'd never recover from. Amazing work, if you ask me, but then I've always had a soft spot for Deputy Joe. Didn't think he had it in him."

He doesn't. Doc wanted to scream. Joe was everything that was good in the world. He didn't drink, Doc had never heard him cuss although he was sure he did. Joe followed the rules and did his job with a quiet strength a lot of shifters in town appreciated. He was fair and yet he was always ready to hear both sides of a story. In the years while his uncle was sheriff, deputy Joe was the one ray of decency in the police department.

"I'm surprised I didn't see the young deputy in my surgery, if he was as injured as Forest says," Doc said carefully, making sure not a shred of emotion showed on his face. He pulled his wallet out of his jacket to pay for the stamps. "Most people don't think anything of knocking my door down in the middle of the night for a scratch."

"It wasn't a scratch, he was gored." Mrs. Hooper looked around, but no one was paying them any attention.

Leaning over the counter, she said in a low voice. "You didn't hear me say this because that young buck has got more pride than sense. Word has it, that young wolf, Mal, went round to see Joe at home the next day because he still had the cruiser. I mean, we all know shifters heal pretty much anything when we shift but Mal caught him stitching himself up. Said he looked as white as a sheet but when Mal ordered him to come and see you, Joe refused. Said he'd quit his job if Mal tried to force him. Mal made him take a week off instead and told him to make sure he had someone with him at all times. That sad-sack Quincy was looking to kill him specifically and you can bet your bottom dollar, there'll be more of that poisonous herd gunning for him now the old man is dead."

"For fuck's sake!" Doc regretted his outburst the moment it left his mouth, but fortunately Mrs. Hooper misunderstood.

"I know, right. I was just as shocked as you are. But those bloody buffaloes have got rocks for brains. I mean, even if they kill poor young Joe, it's not as though anyone's going to let them back into town anytime soon. Arrowtown is well rid of them all, in my opinion."

Doc was sure he muttered some sort of agreement, but frankly he couldn't get out of the store fast enough. The only thing in his mind was the picture of the young, beautiful deputy, sewing up wounds in his own tanned skin. Moving away from the store, Doc looked up and down the street, his fists clenched. The need to see Joe with his own eyes wasn't something he could ignore. There was just one problem. He didn't have the man's address. Joe never visited him as a patient, and Doc never asked around for it, because he knew if he did know where his mate slept, he'd be haunting the house like a pathetic ghost. His mind wasn't helping matters.

Leave it alone. Go back to work. There'll be patients waiting.

He stitched himself up. I bet he didn't even wash the wound or use a sterile needle.

He's a shifter. He won't die from a cut in the gut.

He's on his own. There're killers after him. He's injured, and he won't ask for help.

He won't ask for help because of what I said to him. That thought alone was enough to bring the Doc to his knees and before he knew where he was going, he was on his way to the police station. Mrs. Hooper would know where Joe lived – she knew everything about everybody. But Doc was too afraid he'd break down and tell her the truth if she asked why he wanted the boy's address. Nope, he'd get it from Mal. He had every right to ask for it. He was the only medical professional in Arrowtown and it was his job to watch out for the welfare of every person in town.

Unfortunately, his professional resolve crumbled as soon as he strode through the front door of the station and saw Mal laughing at his desk, Rocky and Liam perched on the corners. If they were all together, then who was looking after Joe? And what the hell did they have to be happy about?

"Doc," Rocky grinned. "What's brought you in here today? Is one of your patients causing you problems?"

"My problem is with you." Doc felt his animal move restlessly under his skin and knew his eyes had changed. "How come I have to hear that one of your own is badly wounded in a fight to the death and he wasn't brought to my office? At the very least, he should've been checked out."

The smile fell off Rocky's face in a blink. "He refused medical treatment. I don't know why but considering how grumpy you are anytime he's gone to your office to interview someone, I can't blame him. Everyone knows you think he's a piece of shit and no good at his job. I guess he didn't want to swallow a lecture on buffalo stupidity along with his treatment."

Doc blinked rapidly and mentally counted to five. "Deputy Joe is a duly sworn officer who works for this town. Under town laws, after sustaining an injury, he has to be cleared for duty by a medical professional. The only shifter medical professional around here is me."

Rocky and Mal exchanged worried looks. Surprisingly, it was Liam who spoke up. "Joe might have refused to go and see the Doc, but there's nothing to stop Doc from visiting him, is there?"

Doc's eyes narrowed as he studied the young lion. *He knows. I'm damn sure he knows which means Joe's told him...but...but....* Mal and Rocky were apparently clueless, and Doc relaxed fractionally. To be honest he was surprised it'd taken Joe this long to crack before telling somebody. Mate rejection wasn't easy to handle alone.

And fuck he is alone and now he's injured and it's all my fault. Doc had never considered a situation where his mate might get hurt doing his job. "I haven't got a problem making a house call, if the deputy doesn't want his image tarnished by visiting my office. Word around town is he's a hero."

"He's more than that." Rocky hopped off the desk and stalked towards him. Doc's animal surged, and it took all his effort not to shift. "Deputy Joe is an integral part of our team. You're right. He's one of ours and in my head, that makes him family. My family. I agree, all of us here would feel a damn sight better if Joe got checked out by you, but if I hear you've said one thing to make him feel bad about what he did, I'll gut you myself."

"What Rocky means, Doc," Mal added, "is Joe's feeling pretty terrible right now as it is. He's killed someone, and worse, that someone was a family member. No matter how horrible old Quincy might have been, family still counts to Joe and he's not taking this death lightly."

"He killed to save me." Rocky was standing chest to chest with Doc now. Doc wouldn't back down, nor would he snap his fangs even though he really wanted to. "He killed one of his family members who was trying to wear my fur as a horn ornament. As far as I'm concerned, he's my brother from another mother. You upset that sweet man any more than he already is, and I'll be wearing your balls on a necklace."

"I hope you've got a bloody strong neck." Doc smirked to ease the tension. "Give me the deputy's address and I'll visit after afternoon surgery. And I promise, not one harsh word will cross my lips."

Rooting around on the desk, Mal pulled out a piece of paper and scribbled on it. "You can let us know in the morning when he will be fit for work, in your professional opinion."

Taking, rather than snatching the precious piece of paper, Doc nodded and walked out. As he made his way back to his office, his mind was running nineteen to the dozen. *Dinner,* he decided. *I'll take him dinner. Fuck. Do buffaloes even eat meat?* Deciding to research buffalo eating habits in between patients, Doc mentally prepared himself for his afternoon work. Six o'clock couldn't come fast enough.

Chapter Three

"Sugar shoots and popsicles." Joe dropped his sanding block with a yelp and clutched his side. It was official. He hated being on leave, sure he was being punished for something that wasn't his fault. And okay, maybe his side would've healed better if he hadn't decided to redecorate his spare room. Boredom had a lot to answer for. He gingerly pressed over his stitches and winced.

"Fuck. Now I've got dust in the damn wound." But Joe was worried more than dust was causing his discomfort. When the wound was still open after a full day, he shifted again really quickly, managing to shift back before he got too far down the road. His buffalo was a persistent beast and wanted to see the Doc and it had nothing to do with his injuries. But even after the shift, the gash was still open and deep. Joe had to suffer through putting in a second set of stitches. Three days later, and the skin was finally closing over, but the red radiating from the wound was not a good sign, nor was the swollen skin around it.

"Shifters don't get infections," he told himself crossly as he made his way down the hall to his bathroom. A peer in his bathroom cabinet made him grimace. He was almost out of disinfectant. He'd gone through a pint of the stuff, trying to ensure he wasn't making his condition worse. Grabbing a washcloth and the disinfectant, he dabbed at the wound, biting his bottom lip as it stung.

"I probably should've showered first," he muttered to himself, noting how the swiped disinfectant cleaned a swathe through the dust on his skin. In all honesty, he was too tired to even think about getting clean. Throwing the washcloth in the hamper, he put the cap back on the disinfectant and then wandered out into the kitchen.

"I'll eat…ugh." Joe peered into his fridge. He needed food supplies as well. He knew Mrs. Hooper would send a delivery with one of her sons if he called. But that would mean talking to someone and he wasn't ready for that yet. "Cheese on toast it is then."

Grating the cheese, Joe found his mind wandering again. It'd become a habit over the past few days. His sleep was tortured with memories of his Uncle's dying gurgles, the blank stare in his eyes. If his nightmares didn't haunt him, the pain in his side did. He was tired, deathly tired, and why he thought renovating a spare room he'd only done over the Christmas break was beyond him. But he had to keep busy – had to keep moving, because if he didn't, he thought about things he'd rather forget.

I need to get a life. Joe knew there was more to life than working and sleeping. But it wasn't as though he'd had the chance to make many friends. Being Sheriff Quincy's nephew hadn't done him any favors, no matter how hard he tried to prove he wasn't like the rest of the family. *Maybe I need to find another shifter town – ask Rocky for a transfer.* But Joe knew he couldn't do that either. Hard as it was, dealing with Doc's rejection, at least he could comfort himself knowing where the man was, and he was safe.

"Ow, fuck it, fuck it, fuck it, fuck it." Joe stared at where the grater had taken the skin off his fingers. All at once his vision blurred and his chest heaved. Cradling his fingers, Joe sank to the floor again, crying as though his heart was broken. And it was. Joe wasn't sure how much more he could take.

Joe didn't know how long he remained curled up on the floor. A sharp knock at his front door had him lifting his head. All at once he was embarrassed at the state he was in.

What if it was Rocky or Mal come to check on him? "Go away, I'm fine," he yelled, his voice hoarse from crying. His stitches pulled as he used the counter to drag himself to his feet.

"Joe? Deputy Joe? Are you all right?"

Sainted mother. Joe would know that voice anywhere. He looked down at his dust covered torso, the black stitches and the inflamed wound. He knew without the reflection in the stainless steel coffee pot that his hair was a tangle of knots and his eyes would be all red-rimmed and puffy. *He can't see me like this.*

"I'm fine. I don't know what you heard, but there's nothing wrong with me. Go away." *I can't face your rejection now on top of everything else.*

"Joe. Let me in. I need to talk to you." Despite his aches, pains, and the mess in his mind, Joe's cock still made a valiant attempt to rise.

"It's not a good time," Joe said frantically. "Call me. We can talk on the phone." Joe thought he could handle a phone call. At least then he wouldn't embarrass himself further.

"Bull-headed idiot," Doc said from the other side of the door. At least, Joe thought that was what he heard, but seconds later his door smashed open, it's lock hanging uselessly in the split door frame.

"You broke my door." Joe struggled to stay standing. "There's laws against that sort of thing."

"You can read me my rights later," Doc said as he came in with a bag in one hand and what looked like a casserole bowl in the other. "Oh Joe, what happened to you?"

I'm having hallucinations. The infection's spread so bad it's tampering with my brain. Because there was no way Doc was holding him upright, stroking his hair, with his bag and a casserole bowl sitting on the counter beside him. But as hallucinations went, it was the best one ever. Joe sank into the comfort offered and cried even though he wasn't sure he had any tears left.

/~/~/~/~/

Doc had broken many hearts over his centuries at life, but when he kicked open Joe's door and saw the state his mate was in, his own heart cracked. Having never seen Joe in anything but his freshly pressed uniform, seeing him shirtless was enough to set his heart fluttering in a most unfamiliar way. But the raging wound on his side, the red eyes, mussed hair and scent of blood – *I don't deserve to have him.* But have him, he would. Any of the reasons Doc had for pushing the young man away evaporated as soon as Joe was in his arms.

Practical needs came first. But which one? This close, Doc's sharp nose could pick up the scent of poison. He didn't need to guess where that was coming from. No wonder Joe's face was as white as the proverbial sheet. But from the heap of grated cheese on the counter, Doc guessed his mate hadn't eaten either. The nasty wound would need to be reopened if Doc had a hope in hell of combating whatever had been lodged in the wound. It would be easier for Joe to handle on a full stomach.

Looking around, Doc spotted a small dining table. Holding Joe steady, he shuffled them over to the closest chair and gently eased Joe into it. When he tried to step back, Joe shook his head. "Not yet. Please not yet."

"Joe." The medical side of him was going to have to insist. "You need to eat and then that wound needs tending to. Just let me heat up the casserole and we'll share dinner."

"Hallucinations don't give orders," Joe mumbled, the arms round Doc's waist tightening.

Crap. I am a fully qualified card-carrying bastard. Doc had never imagined his mate would feel anything but a passing regret that they wouldn't be together. To see, to understand sweet Joe didn't believe he would ever be held by the one fated for him, except as a fucking hallucination cut Doc to the core. Very deliberately he bent down and brushed his lips across Joe's clammy forehead. Then he pinched his shoulder. Hard.

"Ow." Joe pulled back in shock. Then he blinked and blinked again. "You're really here."

"And not before time, looking at the state of you." Doc tried to hide his brusque nature, but it was as ingrained as the gray strands in his hair. "Now please, I'm sure you've got lots to say, but you need to eat, and I've got to lance that wound of yours. Anything else can wait until afterwards."

Joe folded his arms across his chest, his bottom lip sticking out in what could only be called a mulish expression. "I haven't got anything to say to you. You've forbidden me to discuss anything personal with you, and as you can see, I'm not at work, so I can hardly discuss anything of a professional nature."

Ooh, as soon as you are well I'm going to slap your ass rosy-red then fuck it. "I'm sure I deserve your attitude, but that's something else we can discuss later." Doc moved back into the kitchen, collecting the casserole on the way. Popping it into the microwave, he hunted around for plates and cutlery. Joe never said a word, but Doc could feel his eyes scorching the back of his neck.

Five minutes went by far too quickly. Doc placed a filled plate in front of his mate. "I didn't cook this. I fear I don't cook as near as often as I should. But I can vouch for the food.

I pay Mrs. Hooper every week for readymade meals."

Joe flicked a glance at him and picked up a fork, obediently starting to eat. From the speed at which the food was disappearing from the young man's plate, Doc wondered when he last had a full meal. Eating a lot more slowly, Doc scanned Joe's frame. There were a few things that didn't make sense. Like the dust.

"Have you been sanding something?" He asked at last.

Joe looked up from his plate long enough to shrug.

Doc's jaw tightened. "Okay, fine. Take it as a professional question. What have you been doing that has covered you in dust?"

"I needed a project to do because Mal wouldn't let me work for a week. I'm renovating the spare room."

You bull-headed, silly, lonely young man. Doc wasn't blind or deaf. He knew Joe had a rough start in life and working for Sheriff Quincy hadn't helped his position in town. Which is why, Doc swallowed his initial retort and waited until Joe's plate was empty before pushing his aside. "Let me clear this away, and then I'll look at your wound."

"Did you eat before you came here?" Joe looked at Doc's plate which was still half full. Then his eyes widened, and he added quickly, "Sorry. Forget I said anything."

Feeling marginally better, knowing Joe felt the pull to care for him too, Doc cleared away the plates and put the remaining casserole in the fridge alongside the grated cheese he found a plate for. It would make a good topping on toast in the morning, and yes, Doc fully intended on sticking around for breakfast.

Glancing up at the kitchen light, Doc determined it would have to do. "Can you push your chair back from the table, so I can see what's going on with that gash of yours?" He asked, retrieving his bag from the kitchen counter. He'd only brought the basics with him. Hopefully, it would be enough.

Rising slightly, Joe pushed his chair back and fell into it again. His normally tanned face was still pale, although his cheeks were bright red. A quick hand to his brow told Doc it was more a fever than embarrassment induced.

"You've been poisoned," he said bluntly, moving Joe's arm so it rested over the back of his chair. "Is this from Quincy's horn?"

Joe wouldn't meet his eyes, but he nodded tightly.

Doc's blood boiled as he lightly traced the swollen skin, and he couldn't hide the anger in his voice if he tried. "Gods, this is nasty. He tried to kill you."

"What do you care?" Joe pushed his hand away. "If I died it would simply mean there was one less young, dumb, well-hung idiot mooning over you from a distance. You'd never miss me in the crowd of people who all lust after the great Doctor Farriday."

"What are you talking about?" Doc couldn't believe his ears. "I haven't paid attention to anyone in town beyond what's required in my duties as a doctor."

"You don't pay attention to me either," Joe muttered. "I hear a lot in my job and believe me, you're ranked in the top three eligible bachelors in Arrowtown next to Cam and Rocky. Barney and Ra were on the list too, but they're mated now. Every young person, male and female, all hope to catch your eye."

"Well, that's news to me, and it's not as though I have a special pill that will stop people gossiping. Now, don't think you can divert my attention from what you said. If I'd dreamed for a second you could get hurt in your job, I never would have told you to stay away from me. Never. The last thing I want is for you to die. You've got your whole life ahead of you."

"What life?" Joe said bitterly. "I haven't been near another person since I learned you were my mate and that was almost two years ago. Any family I've got left are all trying to kill me and now I'll probably lose my job because I killed someone. Do you hear me?" His voice got louder. "I killed someone. I'm a murderer!"

Shit, this is as bad as I feared. But when Doc tried to put his arms around his distraught mate, Joe pushed him away.

"No. Don't touch me. Don't make me want things I can't have." Joe pulled back as far as the chair would let him. "I don't dare shift because my buffalo would just knock down your door and follow you like a damn puppy. I can't make friends because I'll either have to arrest them, or they're mated like Liam at the office and being around lovey-dovey couples makes me ache for things I can't have. Now, I don't even dare go to town, because everyone there is going to know. They're going to know I killed someone and they're going to hate me. Just leave me. Go. I can't handle anymore. I'm sorry I'm not stronger, but I just can't."

Doc swallowed the massive lump in his throat. Then he did something he never dreamed in a million years he would do. He got down on his knees. "I'm so sorry," he said quietly, looking up at Joe's incredulous face. "Can you ever forgive me?"

Chapter Four

Joe couldn't believe what he was seeing. He'd watched the Doc for years, even before he realized they were mates and knew he was an intensely private and very proud man. There was never any scenario in Joe's head that had Doc on his knees in front of him, not even in *those* dreams. In his head, their positions were always the other way around. The Doc standing above him, feeding his cock into Joe's eager mouth. "Please," he whispered. "Please, get up. There's no way that you should…" he waved his hand at Doc's knees. "That's not right."

"Joe, mate, it's something I would've done a long time ago if I wasn't so proud and stupid. Please believe me, I had a lot of good reasons for turning you away, but, fuck, all I can think when I go through them now, is just how idiotic I've been and how much time I've wasted for both of us."

If he'd been in his right mind, Joe would've protested. He would have demanded to know what all those reasons were and why they were so important. And in time, if Doc was still around, they would have that conversation. But for now, his skin felt clammy and waves of heat were passing through his body. Touching the gash in his side, all he could say was, "please."

Doc was on his feet in an instant. "Come over to the couch," he said softly. "You'll be more comfortable there." Joe felt his arm maneuvered over Doc's shoulder, which was surprisingly broad, as the man helped him stand. Black spots appeared in front of his eyes and Joe clung harder as he felt rather than saw Doc moving him into his sparse but tidy living room. His couch was the one big solid piece of furniture he had in there, and he sank into it gratefully, not sure his legs would hold him anymore.

"Lie down, swing your feet up, that's right." Doc's voice was comforting rather than professional, and Joe let his eyes close as he did as he was told. "Put your arm up here, that's right. Stay on your side as much as possible." Joe felt his head cupped gently as a pillow found its way underneath his cheek. Taking deep breaths, Joe let Doc's scent of ginger and something that reminded him of succulents, fill his nostrils, filling him with a sense of peace he'd never had.

/~/~/~/~/

Doc was livid, even as he let his professional side take over. This close, he could tell some type of narcoleptic had been used. But not just any kind. This was the worst kind of witchcraft, the one designed to kill a shifter no matter how many times he shifted. Joe didn't realize it, but he was lucky he hadn't shifted more than once. While no one knew the magic behind a shifter's ability to morph into their animal form, spells targeting shifters inevitably worsened a condition the more often an individual changed forms.

Working quickly, with a brand new scalpel, just now removed from its sterile packaging, Doc sliced through Joe's remarkably neat stitches and the skin beneath. It was only thanks to years of practice that he didn't gag at the stench and sight of dark yellow puss tinged with black that flowed from his cut. Grabbing a handful of sterile swabs, Doc held them in place with his thumbs as he used his palms to gently press down on either side of the long gash.

Joe moaned, but apart from a tremor running through his outstretched arm, he didn't move. Refusing to acknowledge just how sexy his mate looked stretched out on the couch, Doc pushed on, replacing the swabs every time they became overwhelmed with the gunk coming from his mate's body.

Slowly, but surely, the red swelling receded and eventually, there was nothing further Doc could squeeze out. But the lack of blood flowing from the cut confirmed Doc's suspicions. The narcoleptic still had hold, deep in the wound. His only two options were to surgically remove all the skin and muscle surrounding the gash, or…. *Fight a spell with a spell.*

Swiping the wound clean one last time, Doc quickly checked Joe's vitals. Unbelievably, his mate was asleep, his vitals too regular to indicate any unconsciousness. The sweats had disappeared too, but Doc knew it would only be a matter of time before Joe would be suffering again. He wasn't going to let that happen.

Rubbing his hands thoroughly with some clean sterile swabs, Doc fished in his pocket for his phone. Holding it in his palm, he hesitated. Joe was in a precarious state, physically and mentally. He might not appreciate visitors. Laying his hand over Joe's smooth cheek, Doc said softly, "Joe. Joe. I need you to wake up."

Joe's eyelids fluttered and finally opened. "Did you fix it?"

"As much as I can for now," Doc said. "The poison is a spell, still deep in the wound. What I've done will only bring you temporary relief."

"It's okay," Joe whispered as his eyes closed. "Just let me hold your hand and I'll die happy."

"You're not going to die," Doc said as he picked up Joe's hand and held it anyway. "I need to call someone in to help. Do you know Seth, Ra's mate?"

"The bunny Fae. Yeah. I know him. Your hand feels as good as I dreamed it would."

The way Joe's hand slackened in his let Doc know his mate was asleep again. *He didn't say no,* Doc reasoned with himself, punching out the number he remembered from when

Seth was pregnant. Not many people knew Seth actually died giving birth. But Doc was there. He saw the miraculous recovery the bunny made thanks to his full Fae daughter, Annabelle.

"Ra," he said when his call was answered. "It's Doc Farriday. I need your help…."

/~/~/~/~/

Joe could hear voices. A deep growl, a softer, sweeter voice and Doc. *Doc's still here*. Pushing against the darkness around him, Joe struggled to open his eyes. His eyelids felt as though they were glued shut. He managed to get them open just as he heard Doc say, "You can't use magic on him without his permission. I won't allow it."

"Why did you call us over here in the middle of the night, then?" Ra, or Mayor King as he was now formally known, was standing in Joe's living room, with Seth tucked under his arm.

"I didn't know Seth was going to have to touch him. I thought he could just wave his hands over him or something." Doc turned and noticed Joe was awake. Joe tried to sit up, but a quick shake of Doc's head stopped him.

"It's all beside the point now anyway," Seth said with a grin. "Hi Deputy Joe, I hear you're a bit of a hero around town. We can't go anywhere without someone mentioning your name and there's been three applications to the Mayor's office so far, recommending you for a commendation. Well done."

"You do know I killed someone, right." Joe had to sit up. The mayor was in his living room. "There's nothing heroic about that." He could swing his legs around, but his upper body wasn't co-operating, and then Joe saw why. Doc was holding his shoulder. "Mayor. I would stand up, but...." He inhaled sharply. "I'll understand if you want my resignation."

"Firstly, there's no need for you to call me mayor," Ra said, his deep voice holding a hint of humor. "I was Ra when you stood up to that bastard Quincy and stopped him from arresting me when Seth was being hunted. It's Ra now. And as for asking for your resignation – damn man, people want to put a statue of you on the main street. Do you have any idea how badly your uncle was hated by this town?"

Joe ducked his head. "Yeah, I have a pretty fair idea. I was related to him. I didn't mean to kill him."

"That's because you have a good and decent soul," Doc said fiercely. "I can think of ten other people who'd gladly have killed him and crowed about it afterward. And you're forgetting, you saved Rocky with what you did. That guy is an act first, ask questions later type, but he's good at his job and he'd be sorely missed."

"So, no more talk of resigning, okay?" Seth said brightly. "We've got to get you back to work, and that means healing that crap Quincy's infected you with. Do I have your permission to touch you, seeing as Doc is being so touchy about it?"

"Yes, I guess so." Joe looked over his shoulder at Doc. "Will you be here?"

"I'm not going anywhere." Joe knew Doc was probably just overseeing his recovery, but his heart gave an extra thump, reading a promise that was likely imagined. Closing his eyes, Joe tensed as soft hands pressed against his torso. He wanted to ask Seth if he could mend a broken heart too, but he didn't have it in him to explain why.

Chapter Five

With Joe sleeping peacefully on the couch and Ra and Seth long gone, Doc pottered around the house, doing what he could. He found the room Joe was renovating and swept up the dust and debris fallen on the carpet. In Joe's bedroom, the sweat soaked sheets held traces of blood – testament to the pain his mate had been in. Finding clean linens in the hall cupboard, Doc stripped off the bed and remade it, putting the soiled sheets in the washer to soak. Dirty towels made another load, and when everything was as tidy as he could make it, Doc was back in the living room again.

It felt wrong to just stare at his sleeping mate, but Doc couldn't help himself. Cleaned up, his wound healing properly this time and smelling deliciously of the mown grass and oak Doc craved, Joe was everything he'd ever wanted. *I could have stopped this*, he thought miserably, even while his logical mind argued with him. And in a way, his logic was right. Even if he had claimed the young man, Joe still would have been on duty the night Quincy attacked.

But there would have been differences too. Doc could picture it in his mind's eye. He would have been the rock Joe could cling to as he coped with the killing. Joe's wound would never have gotten so bad. Joe himself...well, he wouldn't have been hiding out in his remote little cabin. Doc would've seen to that. He'd never had let Joe think for a moment the whole town hated him.

I can't let you go this time, he thought as he reached out, curling his fingers in Joe's now clean hair. Seth's magic was a wonderful thing. He'd been unnecessarily cruel to Joe, at the time believing it was in the young man's best interests. But now, he could see how little Joe believed in himself, and Doc was partly to blame for that. He didn't imagine things would all be rainbows and sunshine when Joe woke up, but in time they would be. Doc pulled his hand from Joe's hair and steeled himself as Joe's eyelids fluttered.

"You're still here." Joe yawned and stretched. "What time is it?"

"Around three thirty in the morning," Doc said quietly.

"Three...? You need to sleep." Joe sat up and the cover Doc had wrapped him in fell to his lap. "Why didn't you take my bed? You've got work in the morning."

"I'm fine. I didn't want to be asleep if you needed me for something. But thank you for caring about me."

"I've always cared," Joe looked down at his lap. "A man doesn't stop caring just because they've been rejected."

"Believe it or not," Doc leaned forward resting his elbows on his knees, "A man doesn't stop caring even if he's the one stupid enough to be doing the rejecting. I might not show it, but I've always kept an eye out for you."

"Will you ever tell me why, or is that sort of question still off limits?"

Joe still wouldn't look at him and while Doc knew he was shy, Joe would need to be able to stand up for himself if they ever had a chance at long term.

"Joe, look at me please." Doc waited until Joe raised his head. It was going to take him a long time to get over the guilt he felt when he saw the pain and uncertainty in Joe's eyes. "Joe, I am a very unusual kind of shifter – a rare breed and unfortunately, not one of the glamorous ones." He sighed. "I'm also about three hundred years older than you. It's the age aspect that is one of my concerns. Our life threads join when we claim each other – I didn't want to shorten your lifespan before you've had a chance to truly live."

Doc had to give Joe credit. He didn't just open his mouth and let crap fall out. He seriously thought about what Doc had said. "This life thread concept – who's to say your life thread won't match with mine? Assuming at this point in time, mine is longer than yours."

Frowning, Doc pondered the question. It was a valid one and yet, one Doc hadn't considered before. He'd always assumed he was the stronger shifter, and therefore he believed Joe's life would be cut short if they mated.

"I know you have a lot of strength, in shifter terms," Joe continued hesitantly, "but for a prey animal I'm big and strong in my own right. I imagine, with what you've said about your shifter side, there'd be no comparison between species as such, but surely the Fates, with all their wisdom wouldn't bring you a young mate so late in your life, to cut our time together shorter than it was meant to be."

"I honestly hadn't thought about it that way." Doc tensed. His next revelation was tricky, but he wouldn't take Joe on as a mate unless he was fully informed of all the facts. "You should also know, I've already had a family. My bond mate died a hundred and forty-two years ago next month. I have great grandchildren older than you."

"I'm sorry for your loss." The words were automatic, but Doc could see Joe meant them. "That...er...that does kinda put the age thing into perspective. You having great grandchildren I mean. I've never noticed them in town. Do they ever visit you, or play a big part in your life?"

"I go to visit them once a year, during the summer months, usually for a week. I haven't wanted to leave town the last two years, so made the excuse I was working, but I do keep in contact with some of them, yes."

"You've lived in Arrowtown a long time. For as long as I can remember, anyway," Joe said quietly, and Doc really wasn't sure what his mate was thinking. "Didn't any of them want to live closer to you?"

"My kids all took after their mother. She was a finch shifter. There was an incident with the grandchildren, back when my wife died and while no one was hurt, I felt it best to move away and keep our contact to a minimum. I still send birthday cards with money in them once a year, but I've never been really close to the younger ones."

"That's so sad." Doc thought that was all Joe had to say, but then he asked, "Do you believe your shifted form would hurt me?"

"It's crossed my mind," Doc said honestly. "But when I took the time to see Ra with his mate, and Darwin with his, I started to see things differently. You have to remember, for most of the years I've been alive, shifters mated within their own species and that was it. It was unheard of for anyone to take a mate outside their own kind unless their mate was human and that was often frowned on until paranormals came out. My wife was booted out of her flock for bonding with me. Our children were never accepted by them either. We had to move away and at the time, shifter towns didn't exist."

"That must have been so hard, especially on your wife. I take it, your kind don't live in herds, flocks, or packs?"

"No. We're the kind who will eat each other if food is scarce and the opportunity presents itself. I only considered bonding with Serenity, that was my wife, because I knew she could fly and stay away from my teeth if we shifted together. Your buffalo would be considered prey to my animal."

"At the risk of sounding idealistic, I do believe the true mate bond transcends those concerns," Joe said seriously. "My shifted form is bigger than the majority of other animals and before I knew who my mate was, I worried I'd be the intimidating one in either form. It's why I don't like to shift in front of others."

For a moment Doc didn't understand what Joe meant. He was a big solid young man, but so were many wolf shifters, bear shifters and others. And then it dawned on him and he mentally slapped himself for the added cruelty of his "well-hung" slur. Unsure of what to say, which was a first for him, he fell back on the same argument his mate had used with him. "I have always heard that fated mates are perfect for each other in every way. I can assure you, we'll have no problems in that side of our mating."

Joe's face flushed bright red. "I'm afraid any of my experience in that area is theory based only. I'm sorry if that's going to be a problem."

Problem? Hell no. Doc was ready to dance a jig around Joe's living room at the thought of his untouched mate. But, Joe was twenty-five and a handsome man. The reasons for his inexperience were sobering. Shuffling forward in his chair, Doc reached out and took Joe's hands where they were resting on his lap. "Is mating me what you want? I'm grumpy, set in my ways. I rarely socialize and am pretty much on call all the time, seeing as I'm the only doctor for miles around. My shifted form is big and ugly. If we claim each other, we'd have to spend most of our time living above my offices. Again, because of the on-call reason. I'm not the catch you claim the gossips think I am."

"I'm not a catch either." Joe shrugged. "I have few friends and don't see the point in drinking or making a fool of myself like so many people my age do. My work is really important to me and even when I'm not in uniform, I do my best to conduct myself in a way that won't bring dispute to the sheriff's department. You know all about my family. My parents left town before I could even remember them, leaving me with my Uncle Robert. There're many people in town who still associate me with the wrongs my family did in this town and that's without the added stress associated with me killing my uncle. His family, my cousins and other uncles aren't going to take that laying down. They'll want revenge."

"What I see when I look at you, is a sexily handsome young man, who despite having shit thrown at him all his life, has risen above it and who works hard to keep this town safe. That's what I see in my prospective mate."

If Joe's cheeks got any redder, they'd combust. "What I see in my prospective mate is an intelligent man who doesn't hesitate to ask for help when it's needed. Who's worked all the hours he can to ensure the town is healthy and well, despite his grumbling about it. And someone who totally rocks the sexy silver fox look."

"Would you still think that if you knew I had this?" Doc took Joe's hand and placed it under his shirt. The gray leathery skin of his shifted form was evident in a wide band that ran like a cummerbund right the way around his torso. This was the final test. If Joe didn't go screaming into the night with this, he'd be wearing a claiming scar by first light.

Doc wanted to groan as the heat of Joe's hand gently explored his belly. None of his hookups ever got to see him without a shirt or touch his shifted skin. "Does it go all the way around?" Joe asked, his hand creeping around Doc's side.

"Yes. It's part of my nature as a shifter. My animal is a reptile and our natural counterparts have a few quirks. This is one of the shifter quirks."

"Quirks?" Joe smiled, and Doc realized it was the first time he'd seen that look on his mate's face. It was a seriously good look on him. "Are you…? Nah, it's okay, you'll think I'm being silly."

"No, go on, tell me what breed of shifter you think I am." Doc was mentally celebrating the fact his mate hadn't removed his hand. *He's not put off by this.*

Joe shrugged. "I read a lot and for some reason, I've always found reptiles fascinating. Some of them can be traced back to the time of the dinosaurs, and they are just so different to mammals in so many ways from their habitat to the way they breed."

Fate works in mysterious ways. Doc waited to hear what Joe guessed. He didn't expect him to get it right first time, but his mate had hidden, intelligent depths a lot of people probably ignored. For Doc it was an aphrodisiac as was evidenced by the lump in his pants.

"There was always one type, that fascinated me more than others. I think it's because scientists just couldn't seem to make up their mind about them and they're rare, and terrifying, but I always fancied I saw intelligence in the eyes of ones I'd see in video. The first time I saw you walk from Hooper's store to your office, I was reminded of them then – the sultry way you walk – strength and sensuality all in one. You'll laugh, and I don't mean any disrespect to your animal if I'm so chronically wrong it's not funny. But I think you could be a Komodo Dragon."

For a moment, all Doc could do was stare. Not only did his mate guess correctly, but he thought it was sexy – well, when Doc was on two legs at least. Then he burst out laughing, raising Joe's free hand, the one not under his shirt, to his lips and kissing along the knuckles. "You are a true delight and not only that, but you're the only person in my very long life who's actually guessed correctly. Oh Joe, I'm so sorry I didn't see it before. We're truly made for each other."

"Not so dumb after all?" The twitch of Joe's lips let Doc know he was teasing.

"I've never been so happy to be wrong in my entire life." Doc laughed, and it was as if a giant weight fell from his shoulders. But then reality struck, and he had to be serious one more time. "You do know why I can't tell anybody, don't you?"

"That whole venomous aspect could put some people off from seeing a doctor, I guess."

Doc nodded. "It was bad enough when public perception thought we simply had dirty mouths full of killing bacteria. But when they discovered the venom sacs in the Dragon's mouths, they were feared as much as snakes and scorpions."

"Your secret's safe with me. I promise." Joe looked so earnest and Doc knew his faith in the man was justified.

"Come on," he said, standing and helping Joe to his feet. "You're in no fit state to claim right now, but will you let me hold you in bed? I do need to get a couple of hours before I'm expected at work and yet I find myself reluctant to be apart from you."

"Just don't let go." Joe still looked as though he thought Doc would disappear and his words backed up that expression. "I've waited so long for you to even talk to me in a civil tone, let alone discuss our mating as if it was an accepted fact. I'm still scared I'm hallucinating and you're going to disappear when I wake up."

"If I get a call, I'll wake you and let you know that I have to go and why." Joe would understand the demands of being on call. It was just another way they were perfect for each other.

Chapter Six

Joe couldn't sleep. Not with his mate's arms around him and his scent teasing his senses. His mind churned, going over and over everything that had happened. Joe's torso still ached from Seth's healing, although he felt light years better than he did before. His cock was determined to make an appearance and attract his mate, as was his buffalo, but Joe was well used to ignoring the needs of both. It was what Doc said that was keeping him awake.

Joe felt as though someone had ripped his guts out with a crowbar when Doc said he'd had a family before. Always used to seeing Doc alone, he struggled to cope with the jealousy that surged up in him when Serenity's name was mentioned. But he felt guilt too, that was just who he was. In his head, no one should ever feel jealous of a dead person. There was another shattered dream in Doc's confession. Joe always wanted children, but he didn't feel right mentioning that to a man who barely saw his great grandchildren.

It took every ounce of control to not jump Doc when he got his first feel of the man's abs. The roughness of the shifter skin didn't bother him. In fact, he got a warm glow knowing Doc trusted him, above all other people to know his secret. *You're both loners – who are you going to tell?* His cynical side reared its ugly head, but in a strange way, knowing they were both loners, even if it was for completely different reasons made Joe feel more connected to the older man.

The rustle of a bush outside his window reminded Joe of the other fact he'd learned that night. One that had nothing to do with his mating. Joe couldn't escape the obvious. His uncle had crept into Arrowtown with the full intent of killing him. Coating his horns with a poisonous substance proved premeditation although someone would have had to do that part of things for him. It's not as though buffaloes had opposable thumbs. Joe had to realistically consider who might be after him next. The town's previous mayor, another uncle to Joe, wasn't likely to do anything overt but the ex-mayor had a brother who'd always lived on the fringes of society.

It'll be Uncle Myron, Joe thought decisively. *Not directly – he'd probably send men in to do his dirty work first or a few of my cousins. He's not one to make a direct attack, but it will be him the poisonous substance came from. I'd bet my badge on it.* Analyzing the situation helped give Joe the clarity he'd missed since he'd been injured. It was the only way he was going to be able to keep his mate safe.

My mate. Joe wanted to pinch himself even though his shoulder was still bruised from when Doc pinched him. In repose, Doc looked a lot younger although he still had fine lines splaying from the corner of his eyes. His face was thin, almost as though he didn't eat enough, and his jawline was hard. His eyebrows and scruff were a lot darker than the gray in his hair. Joe had been sorry Doc had used the bathroom to change into a pair of boxers and t-shirt but then he guessed that was more habit than anything else.

It's going to take a while before he can fully trust me with his nakedness, Joe thought fondly, although he was in much the same way. For all Doc's easy acceptance of Joe's fears on the sexual side of their relationship, the man had insisted on sleep rather than claiming him. Maybe he still wasn't sure...maybe....

Stop it! Accept that he's here in your bed now. He wanted to be here. He asked to stay. He begged for your forgiveness on his knees. That has to mean something. It must.

Forcing his eyes closed, Joe tried to sleep. He'd never had anyone in his bed before and he didn't dare move a muscle in case Doc moved away from him. Pale light just started to streak the night sky as he finally dozed off.

/~/~/~/~/

The sharp peal of a phone woke Doc up. He immediately realized he wasn't in his own bed, and it wasn't his phone ringing. *Joe, I slept with Joe,* and it was a good night's sleep too, even if it'd only been a few hours. Reaching over his slowly stirring mate, Doc took Joe's phone off the bedside cabinet and answered it. Whoever was calling had withheld their number.

"Who is this?" He growled in a low tone.

"Doc?" The voice was almost a whisper. "Doc Farriday, is that you?"

Doc immediately recognized the voice. It was the ex-mayor Quincy.

"What are you doing calling Joe's phone?"

"Oh, no. Oh, shit. If you're making a house-call, things must be bad." Quincy sounded panicked even though his voice never rose above a whisper. "Tell me Joe's going to heal. Tell me he didn't get gored that bad? Oh no, it wouldn't matter anyway. One scratch and he'll be dead in days. You've got to do something. You've got to find a way to combat that damn magic serum."

"You knew about this attack?"

"Yes. No. It wasn't my idea. Fucking Robert's gone off his rocker and he's taking the rest of the family with him. I didn't want to do this. I tried to stop him. But he's missing – no one's seen him for days and shit, now you're at Joe's. How bad is he?"

"Why?" Doc snarled, ignoring the question. "Tell me why anyone would do this?" He wasn't about to let Quincy know his nephew was sitting up listening to both sides of the conversation.

"There's a raid planned." Quincy's voice dropped so low Doc could barely hear him. "Soon. I don't know when. Robert wants to take back the town. He's pissed everyone in town voted to throw him out and he's pissed they didn't vote for him the way he expected. He wants his position back. Joe was the only one standing in his way and now he's dying. Fuck. Fuck. Fuck."

"There's a hell of a lot of people in this town who'd stand in his way if he tried anything like that. Rocky, the new sheriff for one thing, or Ra the new mayor," Doc said, infuriated at the idea people he cared about were being threatened. "Your best idea is to turn yourself into the shifter council and tell them everything you know."

"I can't. Robert watches my every move and if he's not around one of his loutish sons is always keeping an eye on me. If Robert comes back and finds me gone he'll kill me."

"If you're anywhere near the town limits Robert won't be the only one you have to worry about," Doc warned.

"No, no. I still own an old camping ground, it was in my mother's name. We're all staying there in the meantime until things can get worked out. It's outside the territory boundaries. I didn't want any of this. You know I always served the town as best I could. I gave that town the best years of my life. I didn't expect the investigation or that we'd lose the elections. Things were good when I was running things, you know that, Doc. I'm sure if the people would just listen to me at a town meeting, I could show them how things would change for the better with me in charge again. It was Robert who was doing all the damage, not me. I just got caught up with things because of the family name. None of this was my fault."

Doc shared an angry glare with Joe, who mirrored his expression. It was typical Quincy would be looking to save his own ass.

"And I suppose Joe was targeted because he shares the same family name, too? Robert deliberately set out to kill him because he thought the rest of the town would roll over and do anything he said with Joe dead?"

"Oh, come on, Doc." Doc shook his head. Quincy used that same tone of voice when he told him his request for funds for an ultrasound machine were unreasonable in light of a declining economy. "I didn't want to see Joe hurt, but how many other big, genuinely threatening species are there in town? A couple of bears maybe, a dozen wolves and most of them could easily be bribed. Robert saw Joe and his insistence in learning and following every single rule in the book to the letter combined with his size the only true threat in town. Joe's too idealistic. He doesn't understand how the real world works. I couldn't stop my brother. Robert's gone crazy. I need you tell people this isn't my fault."

"And here was me thinking you'd only called out of concern for your nephew. If you've got any sense left in that pea-brain of yours, you'll get your ass to the council and confess everything. It's your only chance. I'm not going to do a thing to save your pathetic hide. You make me sick." Doc disconnected the call, put the phone back on the bedside table and pulled Joe into his arms.

"Is there any chance I can take your name once we're mated?" Joe's voice was muffled against Doc's neck, but his arms were a welcome solid weight around Doc's middle.

"Babe, I intend on marrying you as soon as you're ready, and I'll insist on it."

/~/~/~/~/

It was in that moment, Joe understood the importance of a simple hug. In Doc's arms he felt acceptance and compassion and while he knew Doc was angry on his behalf, the man still held him firmly, stroking a warm hand down his back. But that closeness was a double-edged sword. Joe was warring with the instinct to mate. His body was on fire, his nipples tingled, and his cock was fit to burst. But he didn't have the skills or experience to cope with the new feelings. And that in turn set his nerves on edge and made him tense and uncomfortable.

"We need to call Rocky and Mal," he said pulling his head from the haven offered by Doc's neck. "And Ra. They need to know there's a threat to the town."

"Quincy still thinks Robert's alive. Probably thinks he's skulking around here somewhere drumming up support for his return, bribing all the wolves and other predators in this town he dismissed as not important. No disrespect to your fine animal half, but Quincy always had a herd mentality. It's still early. We can afford to wait a few hours before wrecking everyone's day."

Joe's body quivered as Doc's hand moved with more purpose, rubbing over his buttocks and then settling on his hip, dangerously close to Joe's excitable cock. "In the meantime, I think you and I have a more pressing need, don't you? Or have you changed your mind about us claiming each other?"

"Of course, I want you." Joe was shocked to think his mate would think otherwise. "I wanted you before I knew you were my mate. If you walk away right now, that'll never change. You'll always be it for me."

"Your heart is the truest and most honest in existence," Doc said softly, and Joe found himself lost in his mate's dark eyes. "I will cherish that for as long as we're still breathing and beyond." The pressure from Doc's hand on his hip increased. "I want you to lay flat on your back, babe."

"But…but…you'll see…." Joe rolled onto his back, his stomach churning.

"As you'll see me." Doc whipped off his shirt and Joe's mouth went dry. "I haven't been naked in front of someone for more time than I remember." He rubbed across where his gray skin met his tan. "It doesn't look that bad, does it? Sort of like a kinky corset I can't take off."

"You look amazing." Joe could barely breathe, and Doc didn't help when he slid down and then kicked off the boxers he'd slept in. Joe had seen naked men before. It was part of life as a shifter. But the juxtaposition between gray and tanned skin, the surprisingly muscular build; even the dusky pink of Doc's cock bobbing against his gray hide was entrancing.

He swallowed and then swallowed again. Everything in Doc's expression suggested it was his turn. There was a part of Joe that wished Doc would just take the decision from him. Rip off his clothes in a fit of passion, but that wasn't Doc's way. He was waiting. It was a question of trust. *If I'm not man enough to do this, then I don't deserve to be claimed.*

The shirt was easy. Joe didn't think his physique was anything special, but it wasn't anything to be ashamed of. Dropping that garment on the floor, Joe reached for his sleep pants. He couldn't meet Doc's eyes. He couldn't even look in that direction. Doc was going to see him, and Joe couldn't handle seeing anything negative in his mate's expression. Flicking his waistband over his hard shaft, he pulled his pants down and ripped them over his feet. Dropping the pants on the floor too, he lay back and stared at the ceiling.

"Very nice," Doc purred. "I can see we're going to have a lot of fun with that."

Chapter Seven

Like many shifters, Doc never put a label on his sexuality. He'd been perfectly happy, married to Serenity and never felt anything was lacking in the life they shared together. They had three children together and right up until Serenity was taken from him, they'd had an active sex life. In the years that followed, if his needs got too intense, a quick visit to Jackson took care of most of his urges. He didn't care if a person was male or female so long as they were willing to have sex in the dark while he left his shirt on.

But he'd always had a thing for cocks and Joe's was a beauty. Twelve, possibly thirteen inches long, it had a slight curve to the left and the glans were fat and wide. Surprisingly, Joe was circumcised but for Doc that simply meant Joe would be extra sensitive during a blow job especially when he nibbled on those delicious nerve endings located at the base of his glans. Fat balls hanging heavy and low between Joe's legs completed the sensuous picture.

Taking pity on his mate, who was lying as though on a torture rack, his hands fisted by his side and his eyes focused on the ceiling, Doc decided to confront the issue head on, so to speak. Bending over, he cradled the slab of meat in his hands, brushing his lips across the edge of the glans. He was going to have an aching jaw sucking this beast down, but he was willing to take in as much as possible.

"Just beautiful," he whispered, dotting kisses all over the swollen head. A pulse of liquid dribbled out of the slit and he lapped it up, keen for a taste. There was always something musky about a male's ejaculate; musky, salty, but definitely worth swallowing. Joe's thighs trembled as Doc opened his mouth as far around the head of his cock as he could.

Warm flesh. It'd been at least two years since Doc had savored such a thing in his mouth. He rolled his tongue around as far as he could, picking up the nuances of Joe's unique taste. Joe's guttural moan spoke volumes and Doc remembered this wasn't an experienced lover. Tilting his head, Doc stretched the limits of his lips, forming a tight hold just under the flare of the glans and sucked. He was rewarded mere seconds later with more than a mouthful of spunk.

"God's, I'm so embarrassed." Joe had covered his face with his arm.

"I think that takes the edge off nicely." Doc sat up and licked his lips. Stretching out beside his lover, Doc removed Joe's arm, so he could see his mate's lovely face. "Put your arms around me," he ordered quietly. "Learn how our bodies feel against each other."

Joe's groan as he did as he was told was heartfelt and scooted right through Doc's body until it reverberated in his balls. Most shifters appreciated the benefits of touch. Doc, not so much, although as Joe wiggled and found their natural click, he was appreciating it now. Being a herd animal, he wondered how Joe coped with his self-imposed isolation. But it was a fleeting thought.

"We fit together perfectly," he muttered as he catalogued their differences. Joe was broad across his chest and shoulders, but his arm fit snugly under Doc's neck. Their torsos were similar lengths and their legs tangled with a surprising familiarity. Doc rubbed his cock along Joe's length, taking care not to rub too hard. When Joe winced, Doc reached between them, tucking Joe's cock between his legs.

"There's nothing sexy about my inbuilt sandpaper I'm afraid," he smiled.

"I think every inch of you is sexy." Joe's cheeks were bright red. He was staring at Doc's lips and Doc mentally slapped himself. "Have you ever?" He skimmed Joe's lips with his own.

"Not even that," Joe whispered.

"Then let me lead. Breathe through your nose." Doc sealed his lips over Joe's, sucking and teasing first Joe's full top lip and then his slightly fuller bottom one. Joe's hands flailed over Doc's back and then seemed to settle into a rhythm, mapping out both the smooth texture of Doc's shoulders and ass, and the slightly rougher texture of his shifter skin. Doc tightened his thighs and Joe gave a few shallow thrusts. *This boy's a natural.* He flicked his respectable nine inches to one side, so he could take advantage of the smooth grove of flesh along Joe's hip bone and do a spot of rubbing of his own.

Licking Joe's lips, the man opened to him beautifully and Doc was hard pressed not to moan like a two-dollar whore as he dipped his tongue inside. Just that simple touch seemed to spark a passion in Joe, and if Doc was honest, inside himself as well. *Top, bottom? Top, bottom?* Doc usually topped but this wasn't about him. It was about Joe who'd spent his life since puberty worried he was something of a sexual freak. *I sure hope this boy has got a ton of lube.*

"Hmm, you taste delicious," he said, pulling back from their kiss. "Have you got lube, or should I get some from my bag?"

Reaching under the pillow, Joe pulled out an almost new tube. "I use it to bring myself off," he confessed.

"Like most men, I imagine." Doc grinned as he took the tube offered.

"Did you want me to roll over?" Joe looked nervous, and there was a flash of elongated canine teeth peeking from his lips.

"Not this time, babe." Doc put the lube on the bed and held Joe's jaw in his hands. "Sometime soon I will be fucking your ass just as I've dreamed of doing for too many nights to count.

But I want to show you that simply because you're well-endowed, with care and patience you won't hurt your partner."

"But...but...your animal is stronger." Joe looked conflicted.

"We're not just our animals, babe. We're human too. This human has a wide collection of sex toys I pleasure myself with. Usually thinking of you while I'm doing it. The only question I have for you is do you want to prep me, or would you prefer to watch?"

"I want to learn how to please you, if that's okay? I've watched videos but...."

"Perfect, you've got some idea then." Doc rolled over and pulled his knees under him, so his ass was in the air. "There's not much you can do wrong here," he added. "Just don't push too hard. I'll let you know with each finger when to add more." Resting his head on his arms, Doc let out a long breath, so his body was completely relaxed, more than happy to let Joe explore.

Hot, thick fingers rubbed up and down his back, taking in everything from Doc's neck to his butt cheeks and back again. With every pass Joe's fingers got closer to his crack and Doc hid his smile as Joe became more focused on his lower body.

"It's so small and tight." A single finger brushed over Doc's hole, sending a shiver up Doc's spine.

"Babe, I've seen a man take two hands fisted, pounding in and out of his ass and more. Admittedly, it took a lot of grease, and a hell of a lot of time to work that guy open, but the body is amazingly adaptable."

"Have you ever done that? Fisted someone, or had someone do it to you?" Joe's breath skated across his hole and the ends of his hair tickled where they brushed against Doc's butt cheeks.

"I've got centuries on you, babe. Anything I did like that was well before you were born."

"I've seen videos. It just seems so incredible." A tentative tongue dipped into his crack and Doc breathed a little faster. He let out a quiet moan, just to show encouragement, only to feel his butt cheeks pulled apart as Joe's tongue got more insistent.

I don't know what videos you've been watching my precious, but damn I hope you'll watch them again with me.

/~/~/~/~/

Joe had been called a lot of things in his time and most of them weren't complimentary, but anyone who knew him would agree he was a fast learner. Having Doc open to him like he was, was every fantasy Joe ever had come true. Joe didn't have experience to fall back on, but he desperately wanted to make Doc feel good – to not regret having him as a mate. Doc's scent was super concentrated along his crack, making Joe drool and he put that drool to good use, testing with his tongue, the tightness of the muscles around Doc's hole.

When it came to that tight little hole, Joe knew what felt good to him. Of course, he couldn't actually lick his own hole, but he understood how the ring of muscles worked, both externally and just inside the tight space. He alternated, using the flat of his tongue right over the hole until it loosened. Then he rolled his tongue, stabbing at the hole as he held the butt cheeks open.

Doc's quiet moans and the way he wiggled, just a bit, against Joe's hands, boosted his confidence. His own cock hung hot and heavy, bobbing against his leg, but Joe was more focused on bringing his mate pleasure. Smooshing his face right in Doc's crack, freed up a hand and he reached under, touching another man's cock for the very first time.

"Oh, my goodness, babe, you're killing me here." Doc's voice was raspy with sex. "I'm gonna blow if you keep that up. Use the lube and get me ready."

Pulling back, Joe wiped the excess saliva off his chin and reached for the lube. Squirting some on three of his fingers, He used his middle finger to test the softness of Doc's guardian muscle. Doc exhaled as he pushed in and he bit the side of his lip at the warmth he felt inside. He couldn't imagine what that would feel like around his cock, but he was desperate to know.

Later, Joe would thank Doc for making everything easy for him. One finger became two, then three, then four. Rather than push deep, Doc told him to spread his fingers wide in stages. Joe could hardly believe how relaxed his mate was under his attention. But when Doc announced, or rather panted, that he was ready, Joe was hit with an attack of nerves. He'd lived with the terror of hurting someone from the very first tease he got.

"You've done the hard bit, babe. Just don't plunge. Ease your way inside."

Grabbing his cock, Joe looked down at it, Doc's hole and then up at the ceiling. Okay, there was nothing helpful up there. Shuffling forward on his knees, Joe held his cock about midway down the shaft and lined himself up and thrust with his hips. Immediately, the pressure around his glans made him groan. Even Doc's mouth on him couldn't compare.

Everything screamed at him to hold back and he did as he gently eased his way inside his mate. His animal half was a rampant creature full of force and power. But even he recognized the need to care for a mate. Doc was panting hard but rocking back, helping Joe as his cock was slowly engulfed in the heat of

Doc's body. When he'd finally gone as far as he could go he froze.

"Oh babe, you have no idea how delicious that stretch feels." Doc tossed his head from side to side, his long hair brushing over his shoulders. "Just…just give me a minute, if you can. You'll feel the pressure around you relax slightly and that will be your cue to move."

I have to move? Joe was sure he'd blow if he moved one inch. But as he allowed his hands to gently run over Doc's hips, his butt and the band of shifted skin, he took deep breaths to calm himself. Doc was his mate; a man he'd been in love with for two whole years. To have his body under his fingers now; to feel how tightly Doc's body held his shaft captive; this was more than a dream come true. It was the start of a whole new life.

Doc started rocking against him and Joe let him set the pace. He wanted to do more, but it took all his energies not to fall over Doc's back and rut like an animal. *Must not hurt. Must not.* But Doc took the decision out of his hands. Pushing back harder now, Joe got a thrill as he realized Doc was fucking himself on his dick and loving it. Wanting to enhance Doc's pleasure he slipped his hand around his waist and down. Doc's cock was easy to find and fit perfectly in his hand. Testing various pressures, Joe let Doc fuck his hand, while he fucked his ass, letting his various groans guide him.

His balls tingled, and his own butt clenched. Joe knew he was close. The smell of their sex rose up between them and before Joe knew what he was doing, his hips were moving, faster and faster with every thrust.

"Yes. Yes." Doc flicked his hair to one side, tilting his head and exposing the lean lines of his neck. Now, Joe's animal half pushed forward and this time he let him. As Doc met him thrust for thrust, Joe leaned over as far as he could. The brush of Doc's shifter skin teased his gut as his teeth found their mark.

Doc yelled, whether it was a curse or a compliment, Joe didn't know. All he knew was this was the moment he'd been waiting for. He watched with his inner eye as buffalo and Komodo spirits stalked around each other and then brushed together melding as a permanently joined pair. Joe could almost feel the chilly strength of his mate's ancient animal warming against his own, but then he snapped back to his earthly form as his orgasm hit. Sticky warmth coated his fingers as he gently disengaged his teeth, licking over the wound he left with pride.

Giving into his instincts, Joe gathered his mate in his arms and rolled them both, so they were lying on their sides. He buried his nose in Doc's hair, his body still tingling with the strength of his release. Doc's hands came up, resting on his forearms as he pushed his whole body back, as keen for their connection as he was.

"Thank you, my mate. That was everything I dreamed my claiming would be," Doc said softly and within a few seconds Doc's breathing evened out and his body slumped.

For Joe, he wanted to savor the moment just a minute longer. His cock was softening, and he knew he needed to get up and find a washcloth. But for the moment, he had his mate in his arms and he wanted to wallow in the feeling of peace that gave him. Doc was certainly worth the wait.

Chapter Eight

"So, I thought we'd have breakfast in town this morning," Doc said as he drove them both back to his office. He had patients to see, and Joe was going to call in on Mal and Rocky and let them know about the phone call from ex-mayor Quincy. How real the threat was, now Robert was dead, was unclear, but Joe felt strongly his department should be informed. It would be up to Rocky then, if he wanted to discuss it with Ra.

"Together? I...er...I thought you had patients to see. I was going to go straight to the office."

"I do have patients to see," Doc looked over and grinned. "But that's not for another hour. I thought we could sit together, share a meal. It's what mated people do."

"Doc...." Joe twisted his hands nervously.

"I think now we're mated, you should probably call me Nathan."

Joe's eyes widened and then he seemed to give himself a shake. "Nathan, you do realize people in town will hate me for killing my uncle. I'm a common murderer; it was an accident, but a man's still dead. I'll probably get run out of town - banished. Oh, my gods, what will we do then? I bit you. We're bonded. Fates, I should've thought about what this will do to you and your career."

Pulling his car in behind the surgery, Doc turned off the engine and turned in his seat, taking Joe's frantically wringing hands in his. "Joe, no one hates you. You need to believe me. I'm sorry, I should have told you this last night. I heard about you being hurt from Mrs. Hooper when I went to post some letters. The whole town thinks you're a hero for standing up against your uncle and protecting Rocky. Rocky himself told me if I hurt you in any way he'd pretty much bury me. He said he considers you family and so does Liam and Mal. Seth came to your aid at a moment's notice for the same reason. Don't you understand? People care about you and are proud of what you've done."

"But I'm still a Quincy," Joe protested, and Doc could see he wanted to believe, but it was really hard for him. That's what years of self-doubt and insults would do to a person.

"I don't think I've ever heard anyone call you a Quincy," Doc said, trying to remember if Joe had ever been referred to that way. "Everyone in town knows you as Deputy Joe and as far as I'm concerned you're now Deputy Joe Farriday."

"Doesn't mean any of them like me. Doc, Nathan, I'm not doubting your word. I know you'd never lie to me, but most people in town ignore me, unless I'm taking them in for something, or they've got a complaint they want investigated."

"I think you might find that'll change now," Doc said. "If nothing else, they'll know you're my mate and I won't stand for anyone teasing or bullying you. Just as I know," he added as Joe opened his mouth, "you want to protect me too. It's what mates do. It's right up there with having breakfast together. Wouldn't you agree?"

Joe nodded. "I'm proud to be your mate, although there are going to be a few broken hearts drinking at Cam's tonight."

"They're not our concern. The only heart I care about is yours." Restricting himself to just a brief kiss of Joe's knuckles and then a longer kiss on those lips because they were there and as tempting as sin, Doc got out of the car, pleased when Joe came around and took his hand. Doc hadn't cleared him for work yet. He'd asked Joe to take another day off before reporting back for duty, although that was mostly selfishness on his part. He wanted Joe to spend the day with him. But that meant instead of the beige uniform Joe usually wore, he was looking particularly handsome in a pale blue polo shirt and blue jeans that showcased his rounded ass.

Doc was going to have to stop grinning, or people were going to start wondering what was wrong with him, but he couldn't help it. Now he'd gotten over his reservations about mating, he could see just how perfect Joe was for him. Walking along, hand in hand with his mate was the perfect start to the day.

The diner was just a short walk, situated between Doc's office and the sheriff's department. Along the way, people called out, said hello and more than one slapped Joe on the shoulder and winked at Doc as they went past. Joe clearly didn't know what to make of the attention and it didn't get much better in the diner.

"Doc and Deputy Joe?" Hazel, the owner of the diner eyed their joined hands. "Is this a new development or a permanent thing?" A couple of other regulars sitting over by the window, looked up, and one Doc recognized as Mr. Dash, waved and nodded in greeting.

"It's a private matter," Doc said quickly. "But for the record, Joe is my fated mate and we're both very hungry."

Her eyes gleaming with undisguised curiosity, Hazel led them to a table and hurried out the back, probably to spread the news to her husband, George who did all the cooking and their eldest son Lander who worked behind the cash register and generally helped out.

"I was so busy worrying about the reaction to the death of my uncle, I never thought what others might say about us being mates and not acknowledging it before. Just about everyone in town is aware we've known each other for years," Joe whispered as they sat down.

"It's none of their business." Doc kept his voice low too, not that it would make any difference. The whole town would know they were together by lunchtime. It was one of the joys of living in a small town. "But I will step up and tell the truth, that it was my decision to hold off our being together if necessary."

"If anything has to be explained you simply tell them there's a huge age gap between us and you were giving me a chance to experience life to the fullest before you claimed me. That's not unheard of. I'm only twenty-five now." Joe's jaw was rigid.

"We live in a shifter town," Doc shook his head. "They'll scent a lie."

"Then believe it, and it won't be a lie. Look...." Joe broke off as Hazel came over.

"You lovebirds ready to order? Joe, you want your regular?"

"Yes, please, ma'am, and a coffee if you don't mind."

"He's got such lovely manners," Hazel beamed at Doc. "You're lucky you got your head out of your ass and claimed this boy when you did. There's been a lot of chat about your mate's sexy attributes in here over the past few days from both men and women. You could have had competition for your attentions if you'd left it much longer."

Doc knew Hazel was simply fishing for more information, but his grip on Joe's hand tightened. "I never was one for listening to gossip, you should know that by now, Hazel. Joe and I both value our privacy. I'll have the pancake stack with double bacon and coffee, too, please."

Winking at Joe, Hazel sashayed off and Doc let out the breath he was holding. "Now, you were saying?"

"I don't see why people are suddenly interested in me," Joe whispered fiercely. "Sexy attributes, my ass."

"That is one of them." Doc grinned.

Joe's cheeks turned dark red. "What I meant was, in all the years I've been coming here, Hazel has never said anything to me beyond asking me for my order. No one has ever shown an interest in me sexually unless they're drunk and horny enough to fuck a fence post – which is hardly a compliment. Have I got this dangerous edge now it's public knowledge I killed someone? Do they suddenly see me as a bad boy, or what?"

Doc was saved from answering by Lander who came over with their coffee. There was nothing short of hero worship in Lander's eyes as he asked Joe if he wanted anything else.

"No, thank you, Lander." Joe looked up and smiled politely and Doc wondered if he had smelling salts in his bag. The boy looked ready to swoon. He hovered, clearly working himself up to say something but a glare from Doc sent him scurrying back to the kitchen.

"I've never been noticed by anyone before," Joe continued when Lander was out of earshot. "I've worked hard, paid my dues and done my best to live my life right, and I'm ignored. I do one thing, that I struggle to handle and suddenly everyone knows my name."

"Babe, everyone has always known your name. You seriously underestimate your appeal."

Joe arched his eyebrow and Doc's cheeks felt uncomfortably warm. "A lot of my grumpiness towards you in the past was because you're so damn appealing," he growled. "Everyone complains how uncomfortable my treatment room beds are. There's a reason I haven't replaced them, even after all the money Darwin and his friends raised for the clinic. You'll never know how close you came to being claimed over any one of them a number of times."

Joe leaned as close as he could. "I don't care about a bed. You could fuck me up against a wall and the last thing I'd be worrying about was comfort."

Doc heard a little squeak and realized it'd escaped his mouth. He was almost relieved when Lander brought over their food. Apart from some lust-filled looks in Joe's direction, which Joe didn't notice, the food was delivered without incident and the two men were quiet as they ate. That was something else Doc appreciated about his mate. He was quiet and easy to be around – his energies exuded calm and confidence even as he kept a watchful eye on people as they came and went in the diner, and out on the road visible through the large front window.

Doc was just mopping up maple syrup with the last of his pancake when Mr. Dash and another man he hadn't seen around before came over. "Doc, Deputy Joe," Dash nodded respectfully. "I didn't feel it was right to interrupt when you were eating, but as you're all finished, I was wondering...I mean, I hope you don't mind me asking...but...."

"Oh, for fuck's sake, Dash, grow a pair," the stranger interrupted. "You there, you don't look like a deputy anything. What's all this about you killing Robert Quincy? Is that how the law works in this town? Killing people in their shifted form so they don't get a chance to verbally defend themselves? What did you do? Shoot him down in cold blood simply because he got lost and didn't realize he was in Arrowtown territory?"

Joe's face went white, but he very deliberately wiped his mouth with his napkin and set it on the table. "I'm sorry, I don't believe we've met. You are?"

"I'm Justin J. Hargraves, attorney for the Quincy family." Hargraves pulled a card from his jacket pocket, handing it to Joe. Doc did not like the man on sight. His suit was too shiny, his dark hair too greasy and his scent marked him as human. A human who didn't have a lot of respect for shifters, obviously.

It seemed Joe had the same idea. "Mr. Hargraves, I am not sure where you got your information…."

"It's all over town, boy." Doc seethed at the disrespect. "I was in town on a totally unrelated matter, and all anyone can talk about is big, brave Deputy Joe." Doc wanted to punch the man's sneer right back down his throat.

"I don't have to justify my actions to you, Mr. Hargraves, nor do I consider a diner the suitable place to have this discussion," Joe said quietly. "If you have a complaint, then you need to speak to Sheriff Rocky, or Mayor Ra King. However, as you are the Quincy's attorney, then you will also be aware that under shifter law, any banished person found back in the territory he was evicted from can be killed on sight. No one takes the banishment of anyone lightly, and the

Quincy family's removal from Arrowtown was endorsed by the shifter council for their crimes against many people in this town."

"But you're a Quincy too, aren't you, deputy?" Hargraves curled his top lip. "I've done my homework. Who'd you give your ass up to, to keep your job, boy?"

Doc's fists clenched, and Joe gave him a warning look. By now the diner was crowded, attracted by the altercation and the last thing Doc wanted was to make Joe look weak in front of the people he worked among every day. But gods, he wished he had a suture handy, so he could sew Hargrave's mouth shut permanently.

"I'm sure as a well-respected lawyer from Jackson," Joe slowly stood up, "you'd be well aware of the penalties of human involvement in shifter affairs, especially in a shifter town."

"I was retained by the Quincy family who didn't get a fair hearing from this town or the shifter council." Hargraves backed up as Joe reached full height and his adams apple bounced.

"And I'm sure you can explain all of those grievances to the Sheriff in his office." Bending over the table, Joe kissed Doc quickly on the cheek. "I'm sorry my work's interfered with our first breakfast together, especially when I'm off duty. I'll come and find you at your office when I'm done?"

"Looking forward to it, babe." Doc gave his hand a squeeze and then let him go. "Yes," he added for the gathered crowd, "Deputy Joe is my mate, he claimed me this morning." The cheers rang out long after Joe had escorted the pompous lawyer from the diner. Doc wasn't sure who or why they were cheering exactly, but he resigned himself to a busy morning.

Chapter Nine

Joe's sense of calm deserted him as he escorted an indignant Hargraves the two-block walk to the sheriff's building. All those hurtful things Hargraves said. *Is that what the townspeople think? Do they think I killed someone in cold blood? Are they all whispering about how I suck cock, or give up my ass to keep my job?* He didn't think the last part was true. The town had been very vocal about having the other Quincys removed from town and their assets sold. A lot of townsfolk benefitted from it as all the money from the sale was given to those who'd been impacted by the pub raid. Then there was the fact Joe had worked for his uncle for years. If the town had an issue with him still being in town, they'd have made their opposition known at the last meeting about the Quincy situation ages ago.

Like all shifters, Joe could smell a lie and Hargraves reeked of deceit. But when his Uncle Harold rang earlier that morning, Doc didn't tell him Robert was dead and Harold acted scared, as if worried Robert would come back. *So why was a human lawyer in town just hours later, claiming to work for my uncles?* None of it added up in Joe's opinion, and he was happier when he pushed open the door to the building and ushered Hargraves inside. As usual, Mal was manning the desk and Rocky's office door was closed. He was probably napping.

"Joe, I didn't expect to see you here today, but you look a hell of a lot better." Mal flicked a glance at Hargraves.

"Mal, this is Justin J. Hargraves, a lawyer from Jackson, working on behalf of the Quincy family." Joe threw the man's card on Mal's desk. "Apparently, they, or rather Hargraves here, claims I shot my uncle in cold blood, and didn't give him the time to shift and verbally defend himself. If you could take his complaint, I need to see the Sheriff. Is he in?"

"Yeah, sure. Go on in. Mr. Hargraves, if you would like to take a seat?"

"Now look here. If anyone should be seeing the Sheriff, it's me." Hargraves puffed out his chest, which had the unfortunate consequence of straining the buttons on his shirt. "I have important business here. I won't have this boy scurrying in there and undermining my position or working out deals behind my back. He can give the Sheriff a blow job on his own time."

"Oh." Mal drew the word out as he raised his eyebrows. "It's like *that*, is it?"

Joe nodded unhappily while Hargraves gloated. "Ah, I see you didn't know anything about that? Well, let me tell you...."

"Mr. Hargraves sit down! I won't tell you again." Although Mal was physically small, he packed a lot of power in his voice, probably from years of dealing with Rocky. "Joe, go on through. Rocky will be pleased to see you." He gave Joe a sideways glance. "So, is there any chance congratulations are in order?"

Fuck, is there anyone who doesn't know about me and Doc? "Sorry, Mal, you and the guys would've been the first ones I told, if I'd had the chance. Yes, it's official. Doc and I are mated."

"Yes!" Mal held up his hand for a high-five and Joe wasn't the type to leave him hanging. "Rocky owes me twenty bucks. I knew there was something beyond professional interest when the Doc stormed in here yesterday. Go, go, see Rocky. I'll call Liam in as well. Looks like we have a situation on our hands." The look he gave Hargraves was not friendly.

"You have no idea." Striding through the office, Joe kept his spine straight.

Knocking once on Rocky's door, he opened it, not surprised to see the big wolf shifter splayed back in his chair, his head back, his huge boots resting on the desk.

"I'm working, I'm working." Rocky dropped his feet and fell forward. There was a mass of papers on his desk. "Oh, it's you. I thought it was Mal coming in to bust my balls for not submitting the monthly budget forms. Come in. Sit down. How you feeling? Seth mentioned he and Ra were over at your place last night and you weren't looking too good."

"I'm completely healed now, thanks." Closing the office door, Joe sat in front of Rocky's desk. Rocky was a typical alpha wolf, but since being voted in as Sheriff, he kept his long hair tied back and his model-handsome features freshly shaved. He still clung to his jeans and leather jacket though. "Seth was a lifesaver in all honesty. Apparently, someone coated my uncle's horn with some poison or magic or something which was stopping me from healing. By the way, Mal says you owe him twenty bucks."

"You didn't." Rocky groaned and banged his head on the desk. "Do you know how insufferable Mal is when he's right? And you just had to go banging the Doc of all people? I thought you two hated each other?"

"I've known Doc was my fated mate for two years." Joe shrugged. "He had some personal issues that prevented him from claiming me, but we've worked through those problems now. But that's not what I wanted to talk to you about. My uncle Harold phoned me at the crack of dawn this morning."

"The ex-mayor?" Rocky could be serious when he needed to be. "I bet he didn't have anything positive to say."

"That's a bet you would win." Joe went on to explain about how Harold apparently knew about Robert coming to town and how there were more threats coming. "Doc didn't tell my uncle Harold about Robert's death, but Doc and I were in the diner not half an hour ago and some human lawyer, Hargraves, came in spouting a lot of lies and bullshit in front of everyone. He's sitting with Mal now, waiting for me to finish giving you a blow job and he's not happy about me full stop."

"Wait. What? A blow job?" Rocky shook his head, his eyes wide. "Hey, you're a hunk and all that, and I'd flop my cock out for you anytime, but you just got mated and Mal tells me it's not good practice to fuck where you work."

"Mal's right, but apparently that's the only reason I kept my job when the other members of my family were booted out of town. At least that's what Hargraves was telling everyone. Apparently, he's done his homework on me and that's what he's come up with." Joe was still pissed anyone could think he got and held his job for any reason other than the hard work he put in. He'd worked seven days a week, sometimes sixteen-hour days when Rocky first took over as Sheriff and the Quincys were banished. Things eased when Liam was made a deputy too, but then he had problems with his mates, and Joe took up the slack again.

"That insulting piece of shit." Rocky flew out of his chair and stormed out of the office, fur sprouting on his arms. Joe hurriedly followed him. Rocky could be headstrong at times and Mal wasn't always able to hold him back.

"Who the hell are you to come in here, insulting my deputies and this department?" Rocky loomed over Hargraves who shrank in his chair.

"You can't touch me. I'm a lawyer."

"I'm not going to touch you," Rocky sneered. "There is no way in hell you're my type and unlike you, I know how to act like a professional. I want to see your proof, asshole. If you've done your homework on Deputy Joe, then share with the rest of the class, because apparently there's a whole stack of shit going on, I don't know about."

"Is there somewhere we can speak privately?" Hargraves eyed Rocky's office and Joe's buffalo went on alert. But it seems Rocky's wolf was just as canny.

"I trust these men with my life. It's a shifter thing, you're probably not conscious of. But you can speak freely out here. Deputy Joe has a right to hear the accusations against him and the proof you have. Joe, I don't want you making this man feel uncomfortable, so you can sit over there." Rocky perched himself on the edge of Mal's desk and after pointing at the spare seat at the desk next to it which Joe took, folded his arms and waited expectantly.

"Ah, yes. Well." Hargraves didn't look so confident, faced with three shifters. Humans didn't have the same ability to scent like shifters did, but their sixth sense was brilliant at letting them know when a predator was near. Rocky was a powerful alpha and if Hargraves thought Mal was a problem, he was in for a shock with Rocky.

"It's quite simple really," Hargraves said, once he realized no one was going to say anything. "I've worked for the Quincy family, that's Harold and Robert Quincy since they were ousted from Arrowtown on trumped up charges of fraud, creating public endangerment, and embezzlement."

Rocky held up his hand. "Stop right there. The charges against Harold and Robert Quincy were proven with extensive records, eye witness testimony, and bank statements. That proof was accepted by the shifter council who rules on these things and a town meeting was held to determine their punishment, again as prescribed by shifter law. They were lucky all that happened was they had their assets forfeited and they were banished. Some of the other options presented by some of the people in the town would have left you with no one to pay your bill. None of those charges were trumped up as you called them, and this is not a court room. I want to hear your proof."

"Yes, but you see, there was no right of appeal."

"Shifters can smell deceit, Mr. Hargraves," Mal said softly. "On all paranormal and non-paranormal species." The warning was implied, and Hargraves swallowed hard. "Shifters don't need an appeal process because it's impossible to lie to them. The Shifter Council judgements are final as are those arising from full town meetings in a shifter town like ours. I'm sure the Quincys showed you documents of the transcripts of the interviews held with them by the Council."

"They could be in my files. Look, Sherriff, there's still the matter of why your deputy, Harold's and Robert's nephew, is still in his position when the rest of the family – mates, children and all – were banished."

"Deputy Joe has worked for this department for five years. His record during that time has been exemplary. He was investigated as part of a department wide inquiry and exonerated. I believe you have proof he used sexual favors to retain his position?" Rocky's glare was enough to make anyone crumble.

"Not proof exactly, no. I am in town conducting my own research into the situation after Robert's shocking demise. But just look at him. He's not even in uniform. He's dressed as if he's trolling for a pickup."

Joe fisted his hands under the desk but stayed mute. He trusted the people he worked with, and Mal didn't disappoint. "I'd watch what you say, Mr. Hargraves," Mal warned, his soft voice holding a definite edge. "I'm more interested in how you came by the knowledge that Robert Quincy was shot in cold blood, by Deputy Joe, and given no chance to shift and explain why he was on old man Forest's property causing havoc with his sheep. Where did you hear that ridiculous fiction?"

"There was an eye-witness." Hargraves's smug look was back. "I took his statement an hour ago and have it signed legally." He reached in his pocket and pulled out a piece of paper. Rocky held his hand out and Hargraves let it go. "I've got copies," he added as though afraid Rocky would eat the paper or pee on it.

Mal leaned out of his seat to read over Rocky's shoulder. Rocky handed the paper to Joe as both men started laughing. Frowning, Joe scanned the scrawled writing.

I hereby certify was me that saw Joe with a big-assed gun shoot that asshole Robert Quincy. My shifter eyes confirmed everything the sleazy lawyer said. I was there and saw everything.

It was signed with another scrawl and Joe's lip twitched as he made out the letters.

D.G.AF.

"Did you meet Mr….Er..Mr. Af anywhere in particular?" Joe asked, looking up from the confession. "Outside a bar called Cam's by any chance?"

"As a matter of fact, I did. There were a group of men gossiping about poor Robert's death while they were waiting for the establishment to open for business." Hargraves fiddled with the hem on his jacket. "But the eye-witness testimony still stands. Mr. Af signed the paper before the pub was open."

"It's rather sparse on details." Joe couldn't look at Rocky because he knew he wouldn't be able to keep a straight face. "There's no mention of the time of day, the date, or where the witness was when he saw these alleged incidences. It doesn't even mention where the incident took place. As testimony, it's very thin."

"The bar was in the process of opening. Mr. Af told me he had an urgent appointment inside. But he gave me enough for me to insist you instigate an investigation." Hargraves was looking between Rocky and Mal, probably wondering what was going on. It didn't help when Rocky roared with laughter again, slapping his leg and making Hargraves jump.

"I bet I know who his appointment was with," Rocky spluttered.

"This Mr. Af," Joe bit his lip to stop his own chuckles. "I assume he's a local in town? Can you give me a brief description of him please? Just the basics. Rocky, of course, will need to interview him as part of any investigation."

"I may have to call in the shifter council, if this serious matter can't be treated with more respect," Hargraves said tersely. Rocky was leaning on Mal's shoulder and Mal was trying to calm him down. "However, it's of no consequence. All the details will come out during the court case. The witness was a rather short, portly gentleman. He had black curly hair that looked as though he didn't own a hair brush. Black moustache and a gray flecked black beard. His friends called him Dave."

Joe knew exactly who Hargraves was talking about. "And I imagine you gave him money for being so forthcoming? Expenses. Nothing illegal, but a man has to be paid for his time, right?"

Hargraves shrugged. "It's not uncommon in legal circles to reimburse informants for important testimony."

"How much did you give him?" Joe reached for his phone.

"Fifty dollars." Hargraves looked him in the eye as if daring him to say something about the amount.

Joe didn't say anything, at least not to Hargraves. Pressing a contact in his phone, he waited for the call to be answered. "Mrs. Hooper, how are you this fine morning?...I'm a lot better, thank you...I will...I promise...Ma'am, I thought you should know that a lawyer in town...yes, that's the one...he gave Dave fifty dollars about an hour ago. You might want to...yes, your boys can handle it...he's at Cam's. Thank you, Ma'am, I thought you had a right to know. I'll let you take care of it. Thank you very much, Ma'am. You have a lovely day. Goodbye."

"Who's this Mrs. Hooper and what's she going to do to my witness?" Hargraves glared, which Joe ignored.

"Mrs. Hooper's boys will pull Dave out of the pub before the lunchtime rush. She's not happy, but she'd rather do that than pay for damages at Cam's." Joe looked at Rocky.

"The best call to make, this time of the morning." Rocky grinned. "I'm glad I don't have to go and get him."

"Sheriff, I demand to know what's going on with my witness." Hargraves stood up but a glare from Rocky had him falling back in his seat again.

"You don't have a witness," Rocky explained. "You've been conned. I imagine you were walking along and heard the regulars outside Cam's gossiping about your client's death and Joe's heroism that night. Knowing that crowd, you had to flash a bit of money to get someone to talk to you. After all, you're not a local, but money talks in any language, right?"

Hargraves started to look uncomfortable. "Dave is a town icon, I suppose you can call it. Everyone knows him," Mal took up the story. "He's well over three hundred years old and remembers a time well before shifter towns were created. He's also known to go on a bender once in a while and usually causes a lot of damages especially if he shifts. Which is why his long-suffering niece, a powerful woman in her own right, makes sure he has a limited amount of money to spend in the pub every day. I'll bet you that fifty and double it, that if we went to Cam's right now, he'll be sitting holding court with his friends, laughing about how they all got one over on the human lawyer with more money than sense."

"How do I know you're not lying to me?" Hargraves's eyes narrowed.

"The signature and the description, for a start," Joe said, pointing at the scrawl at the bottom of the page. "Your Mr. Af is Dave Hooper, known to us and the shifter council as a bit of a rogue who never does any harm unless he's had too much honey dew beer. Then, you don't want to get in his path. He's a Texas Longhorn shifter with wicked horns."

"But...his name is Dave. Why sign his testimony as Mr. Af?"

"Don't Give A Fuck." Rocky chuckled.

"I beg your pardon."

Joe pointed to the signature again. "It's Dave's customary signature if you ask him to sign or verify anything that he thinks is a pile of shit. D.G. Af. It stands for Don't Give A Fuck." Opening the desk drawer, Joe hunted through the papers, looking for Dave's last arrest form. "Here, you see? Is that the man who gave this testimony?" He pointed to the photo at the top of the form.

Hargraves nodded, his cheeks going bright red. Dave's arrest photos always had him flipping the bird at the camera. "And this is his signature at the bottom of the form. See, they are exactly the same."

"I want that man arrested!" Hargraves jumped to his feet. "He stole from me. He's nothing but a bald-faced liar and a thief."

"Dave didn't steal anything from you." Rocky got to his feet as well. He was at least a foot taller than the lawyer. "It says in his testimony that he was confirming what you told him to say. You paid him for that. In this town we call that a fair exchange. Now, that's out of the way, I demand to see the proof you have regarding Deputy Joe's use of sexual favors to keep his job." All signs of humor had left Rocky's face. "That is a serious accusation and one that reflects badly on everyone in this department."

"No," Hargraves blustered. "What is a serious matter is Joe Quincy killing his uncle in cold blood. Shifters don't use guns – you all consider that a sign of weakness. Well, that's what Joe Quincy did, and Harold Quincy and Robert's sons are calling for restitution as defined by shifter law."

"I knew this would be about money," Joe sighed. He wished Doc was with him. Being away from a mate wasn't easy for any shifter, and Joe hadn't had his three days with Doc as was allowed for a new mating. "Mr. Hargraves, exactly how did you come to the conclusion that Robert Quincy died from a gunshot wound? I understand how you came to find out I was the one responsible for my uncle's death – everyone's talking about it. But what made you think guns were involved?"

"I...er...it'd have to be a gun. Deputy Joe doesn't have a mark on him." The scent of nervousness filled the air and Hargraves gulped.

"Shifters heal quickly as a rule. If Joe got scratched up or injured in a head to head fight, then he'd be already healed – unless there was something

156

on Robert's horns that prevented him from healing. You know something about this!" Rocky smacked his hand on the arm of Hargraves' chair. "You knew about the magic used to try and kill my deputy."

"No. No." Hargraves was pulled back in his chair, but he had nowhere to move and the stink of his deceit filled the room.

"Don't you lie to me, you piece of shit," Rocky snarled, showing his fangs. "Four nights ago, the Arrowtown sheriff's department responded to a call from Forest who said a buffalo shifter was on his land, terrorizing his prized sheep. Deputy Joe works nights, something Robert Quincy knew. When Robert wouldn't shift, despite repeated calls for him to do so, as witnessed by three other individuals, Joe – the only one capable of running him off – shifted and Robert attacked him. All Joe was doing was trying to get Robert to run off, but Robert decided to pick on someone else, smaller than himself and Joe. Joe, at great personal cost to himself, made the killing blow to save that other person's life. During the course of the fight Joe sustained a major injury – an injury that until last night brought him close to death."

"I'll need to speak to those witnesses," Hargraves bluffed.

"You're speaking to them." Rocky pointed to himself and Mal. "And if you're sleazy mind thinks this is a conspiracy, go and talk to Forest yourself, or Seth the half Fae who saved Joe when nothing else would work. They'll gladly talk to you when you get out of jail, that is."

"Jail?" Hargraves squeaked. "I'm a lawyer, you've got no cause to hold me."

"At approximately 5:52 this morning, Harold Quincy called me." Joe leaned over the desk and fixed Hargraves with his glare. "I didn't answer the call, my mate did, but thanks to shifter hearing, we both heard the entire conversation. Harold thought I was dying. My mate's a doctor, so it was a fair enough assumption. Harold knew about the poison. Yet you came to the diner to find me. Harold said Robert was crackers and planning to take over this town by force if necessary. He didn't know, at 5:52 this morning that Robert was dead. Three hours later and you're in town discrediting me and spouting lies in front of dozens of witnesses who could all smell your deceit."

Standing up, Joe flexed his arms and shoulders and then rotated his neck. "My mate will be wondering where I am," he said to Rocky, ignoring Hargraves completely. "This shit interrupted our first breakfast together. If it's all right with you, I'm going to make it up to him by taking him lunch. My recommendation, as a humble deputy, is that Justin J. Hargraves be held for further questioning and possible interrogation by the shifter council investigators. There're severe punishments for humans who involve themselves in shifter affairs and his behavior in the diner - defamation of a public official in front of a dozen witnesses - should be enough to hold him until the council gets here."

"There's nothing humble about your legal knowledge, Deputy Joe," Rocky laughed. "Go, spend time with your new mate. I think I might give Simon a call."

"Simon? Darwin's Simon?" Joe tilted his head, thinking about the snake shifter. Then he remembered Simon was the only lawyer in Arrowtown and his shifted form was both impressive and lethal. "That's an excellent idea, boss. Far be it for us to deny our prisoner legal representation. Now, if you'll excuse me." Nodding at Mal who was grinning wildly, he headed for the door, stopping just before opening it.

"By the way," he said over his shoulder. "If Simon finds out, in the course of his investigation, who has been spreading it around town that I give up my ass to keep my job, let me know will you? I think that particular crime is one handled personally, don't you think?"

"Let me know when and where, my friend, and I'll bring the shovel." Rocky grinned but when he turned back to Hargraves his grin was feral. Smiling, Joe headed outside, more than happy to let Rocky and Simon handle that piece of shit Hargraves. He was desperate for some alone time with his mate.

Chapter Ten

"I'm sure this scratch will heal with a simple shift," Doc said for the tenth time that morning. Bent over Chuck Branston's arm, he dabbed at the jagged scratch with some alcohol. It didn't even need a band-aid. "What is it you really wanted to see me about?"

Chuck was one of the many rabbit shifters in town. He was a nice enough boy of about twenty, with blond hair and bright blue eyes and a fair skin that showed every one of his blushes. "I was worried about my arm but seeing as you asked. Lander over at the diner said you'd been claimed by Deputy Joe. He's pretty upset about it. He's been trying to work up the courage to ask the deputy out for months. A bit like me."

"You wanted to ask Joe out too?" Doc wasn't surprised Joe had his own fan club. Just because he didn't partake in gossip didn't mean he didn't hear it and he'd spent two years frustrated every time he had to listen to someone else drool over the way his mate looked in his uniform.

But maybe Chuck wasn't part of that group as he shook his head. "Ew, no, that would be too weird, with Lander lusting and sighing over him all the time." He tilted his head shyly. "I'm kinda into daddy figures myself. So, I was wondering...."

Doc straightened his spine and glared. "Whatever you were going to say, don't. I might be ancient compared to you, but I'm not anyone's daddy. Joe is my true mate and that is the only reason I allowed him to claim me."

"Nah." Chuck grinned. "There's no need to pull my leg, Doc. I can take a hint. Silver fox like you, I bet you've got a dozen men stashed in your apartment lusting after you. If you knew Joe was your true mate, you guys would have done the humpty dumpty years ago. Fuck, he must be close to thirty or something so you both had to know. Come on, you can tell me, I won't tell anyone."

Only a dozen of his friends and then countless others on social media, Doc thought drily. "The truth of the matter is, I'm a right asshole. I made Joe wait because that's the kind of bastard I am. I was damn lucky he forgave me, don't you think?"

Chuck wriggled his nose as he sniffed. "Shit, you're not lying. I mean, yeah. If my mate ignored me for years, I wouldn't let him bite me if he begged me."

"And that just goes to show what a saint Joe is. So, you can tell your friend Lander and anyone else who thinks they have a chance at my hunky deputy, to keep their hands off. Understood?"

"Yes, Doc, although Lander's going to be devastated." Chuck jumped off the bed with the exuberance of youth and headed for the door.

"And Chuck, next time you want to deliberately scratch yourself, make sure you use a new nail. Rusty wounds can go septic really quickly and that's without the peril of lockjaw."

"You're full of jokes today, Doc. Mating must agree with you." Chuck skipped out the door leaving Doc shaking his head. Thankfully, the dangers of tetanus weren't common in shifters as they generally shifted to heal any minor wounds. "He could have just talked to me in the first place," Doc muttered as he disposed of the dirty swabs and then went out to the waiting room. A man and two women looked up at him expectantly.

Sighing heavily, Doc said, "Do any of you have any major injuries, or were you just here to quiz me on my mating with Deputy Joe? Because if it is information you're looking for it would be a lot quicker if I just answered your questions now as a group, and then we can all get on with our day."

The people in the waiting room all looked at each other.

"Just as I thought." Doc crossed his arms. "Deputy Joe is my fated mate. We've both known about it for years, but I was being an asshole and refused to accept his claim for a variety of reasons which are personal. When I knew Deputy Joe had been severely hurt in his altercation with Robert Quincy, I realized, like an old fool, that being with Joe was all I wanted, and I begged his forgiveness. Like the patient man he is, Joe forgave me, he claimed me and that is the end of the matter. Anything else?"

"Is Deputy Joe all right now, Doc?" Mrs. Hannah from the clothes shop asked. "My Errol said he looked peaky this morning at the diner. A growing man like that needs his food."

Her friend, Betty who ran the hair salon nodded. "Joe's always been a good boy. You're going to have to take care of him, Doc. Lord knows, his own family spit on him every chance they got, and that boy needs some loving."

"I'll be sure to meet all his needs, ladies. He is very special to me. Now is that all?"

"Well, I think I got an ingrown toenail." Dan, the beta wolf who ran the hardware store pointed at his boot. "I didn't know you was mated, so congratulations. But what about my foot?"

"Come on in, Dan, and I'll take a look at it. Ladies, you have a nice day and feel free to pass on what I said about my mate." Doc nodded at the two women who were gathering their things and indicated for Dan to go into his treatment room. As he closed the door, he looked up at the clock. Joe had been gone over an hour. Rubbing away the pang in his chest and forcing down his animal's anxiety, Doc pulled up his rolling stool as Dan sat on the edge of the bed. "Get your boot off, and let's take a look."

Poking around what was indeed an ingrown toenail, Doc was surprised when Dan suddenly spoke up. From memory, he'd only spoken a dozen words with the man in years. "What's it like, finding your true mate?"

Doc looked up, but Dan was staring at an eye chart on the wall. "It's like a punch in the stomach," Doc said focusing his eyes on the inflamed toe. "You catch a person's scent, and all of a sudden you can feel it all over your body. Your animal wants to break free, your cock goes nuts and you know your life is about to change forever."

"I've never had that," Dan said so softly Doc strained to hear. "It's my nose. Something happened when I was a pup. I've never been able to smell anything. There's this lady, she's a rabbit. Jenny is her name. She makes me feel all of the things you said, but I can't smell her and it's not as though I can ask her if she can scent me. Then she'll know, you know, that there's something wrong with me and I don't want her to find out."

"You've had this problem as a kid and you've never said anything to me?"

"Well, a man doesn't like to talk about these things." Dan winced as Doc probed a particularly sore part of his toe but hid his discomfort just as quick. "It's not something I've really worried about. Sometimes, not being able to scent anything's been a blessing in disguise, you know, when I've been in the pub some nights. I don't hunt in my fur, and I never imagined I'd meet my mate. But then I saw Jenny and now...you know what I mean, being mated yourself."

"It consumes the brain, that's for sure." Doc snipped and yanked out the offending piece of toenail. Dan barely flinched, but then beta wolves were built tough. Dabbing at the spot of blood that welled up on the side of Dan's toe, Doc could see it was clotting already. "Your toe's fine now, but if you lay back, I'll take a look at your nose for you."

"You won't tell anyone, will you?" But despite his worry, Dan lay down quick enough. "It's just, I lost my pack already because I can't smell anything, and I like my life here."

"You know me better than that," Doc snapped back. "Think how much better your life would be if you had Jenny in it."

"She is so pretty," Dan stared at the ceiling while Doc ran his fingers along the top of Dan's cheek bones. "She's got a real softness about her and every time I see her, it's like the sun comes out even on a rainy day."

Doc tried to hide his smile, but it wasn't easy. He could empathize with the way Dan felt. He used to think

Joe walked around with his personal spotlight, the way he seemed to glow every time Doc saw him. He was all focus though when he felt a small lump that shouldn't be in Dan's sinus cavity, very close to the nose. Pressing gently on the other side of the nose, he noticed it was there too. It couldn't be a complete blockage, or Dan wouldn't be able to breathe, but there was definitely something there.

"When you fell, when you were young, did you see a pack doctor or anything like that?" He asked, grabbing hold of a small pair of forceps and his pencil torch.

"My mom said my nose bled for ages, but when it stopped she figured it was just like a normal bang, you know. I was only about four at the time. I didn't even realize I couldn't smell anything until puberty hit me and I shifted for the first time."

"I think the fall dislodged a tiny splinter of bone from your skull, or cartilage or something, and in those years between when the fall happened, and you shifted for the first time, calcified deposits grew around the initial impact and slowly reduced your ability to smell. I imagine food doesn't taste that interesting either."

"Never knew what the fuss was about it," Dan chuckled. "My stomach tells me I'm hungry and I eat, but yeah, I don't really enjoy it the way I see other people do."

Examining all he could without being too invasive, Doc sat back. "The good news is I could do surgery to remove the blockage. The problem is, because the damage happened when you were really young, it could take months before your olfactory sensory neurons, the things inside your nose that connect to the brain and tell your brain what something smells like, start to work again. There is also a chance they're permanently damaged and the surgery might not work at all."

Dan's face fell. "How will I be able to find out if Jenny is my true mate? If I keep putting her off, she's going to think I don't want her and I do."

Doc was useless as a counselor, that was why he studied as a general practitioner, and then later as a surgeon. He didn't have the time or patience to help people with their emotional problems unless they could be solved with physical treatment. But he felt a rush of compassion for Dan. *Damn mating hormones.* "Dan, this is strictly between you and me, all right? You tell anyone I am dishing out advice and I'll deny it."

He waited until Dan nodded before continuing. "What I think you should do is take Jenny out on a date. A private date. No relatives or friends and make sure it's somewhere nice – maybe in Jackson so you can have some privacy. Buy her a lovely dinner, remember rabbits aren't big meat eaters so make sure they have salad on the menu. Then, explain what happened to you."

"Now wait," Doc said quickly as Dan's eyes widened. "If she is your mate then she deserves the truth. She's also a shifter. She will know if you two are mates or not, because she will be able to scent you. In fact, I think it's safe to say that if she accepts your dinner invitation then you can pretty much guarantee she is your mate. Contrary to popular belief, most shifter rabbits don't engage in casual sex. They wait for their mate, so if she says yes to dinner, then there is a good chance the rest of the signs your body was telling you were right."

"No one else in town knows except you," Dan protested. "What if the other wolves start giving me shit if it becomes public knowledge?"

"Do you really think Jenny would do that to you? Spread gossip all over town like that?"

After a long minute, Dan shook his head. "No. Jenny's not like that. She's quiet and spends more time in the library than going out with friends."

"Then you need to take a chance. I mean, I could do this operation and it could work and then your sense of smell would be restored. But that could take a while and, in the meantime, if Jenny has scented you, then how's she going to feel, thinking you know you two are mates and so clearly don't want her?"

"She'll think I'm being the same sort of bastard you'd been with Deputy Joe," Dan chuckled. "Yeah, you're right. I can't sleep for thinking about her. I don't know how you held out for years."

"I spent a hell of a lot of frustrating time with my right hand," Doc grinned to show he was teasing. "Talk to Jenny, ask her out on a date and then, if it all works out, you can both come and see me, and I'll explain about the operation, what's going to happen and how it might help with your sense of smell. You don't want to miss the scent of her being pregnant with your pups, do you?"

"Aw, fuck, Doc. Now, I'm not going to be able to stop thinking about it." Dan sat up and swung his legs off the bed. "You're a persuasive old coot, you know that?"

"Whatever works. Good luck with your dinner."

Dan had barely been gone a minute and there was a tap at the door. "Yes?" Doc was jotting down some notes on what he'd found and treatment options for Dan. He looked up to see Joe poke his head around the door. His mouth stretched into a genuine smile and his cock firmed underneath his white coat. "Joe, I've been worried about you. Come in, come in."

"I wasn't sure if you had someone here with you," Joe opened the door to reveal a large covered tray he was holding in one hand. "I brought you lunch seeing as our breakfast was ruined by my work."

Doc's heart melted. He knew it wasn't physically possible without external application of heat, but that was exactly what it felt like – his solid heart muscle oozing like a melting ice cream. Standing up, he met Joe halfway, taking the tray from his hand and putting on the nearest stainless steel trolley. "My work is bound to interfere with our lives more often than not, too, babe. I'm not upset by what happened this morning. I'm just so freaking glad to see you." Cupping Joe's jaw with both hands, he pulled his young mate closer for a much needed kiss. His ass clenched as he felt Joe's arms wrap around him, his lips yielding to his. *I need to get a more comfortable treatment bed.*

Chapter Eleven

Joe had been nervous, entering Doc's inner sanctum as he did. Any time he'd been there before, working on a case, Doc had scowled at him as though he'd shit in the man's dinner plate and treated him like crap. He'd do his job, usually questioning someone, with Doc glaring all the while and then Joe would leave, his heart splitting in two every single time he walked away.

Doc's smile helped ease his tension, and his hot kisses, as though Doc had missed him too, turned that tension into something far more palpable – pure, intense need. Joe still wasn't sexually confident. One night of passion didn't make him an expert, but he was a quick learner, and this was a scene he'd dreamed of a hundred times. Sliding his hands down, he slipped them under Doc's long white coat, eager to feel his mate's body underneath.

"Don't rip it," Doc warned as he pulled back from their kiss. "Strip off."

Joe cast a worried look at the door.

"It's got a lock, use it and then get out of those clothes." Doc was busy undoing his coat. Joe hurriedly went over and locked the door, pulling his shirt over his head as he came back. Boots slipped off easily, but his jeans were a bit more awkward. *Why did I have to wear my tightest pair? Oh yeah, because I wanted my mate to be proud to be seen with me.* But not even the strongest of denim was safe under his fingers, and Joe dumped his jeans on top of his boots and looked up, quickly swallowing the drool that pooled in his mouth at the sight of Doc naked and waiting for him.

"I'll never get used to seeing you like this," Joe whispered as he moved forward, his arms outstretched. "I've dreamed of seeing you in this office, exactly like this, too many times to count."

"Were you pulling yourself when you had those dreams?" Doc's hands on his cock were heaven.

"Every single time." Joe knew his face was red, but the glaring white scar on Doc's neck reassured him – reminded him they were mates and Doc wouldn't turn him away again. "I've always wanted to do so much with you even when I didn't know what I was doing."

"Did you imagine this for example?" Doc sank gracefully to his knees. "Or maybe this?" He licked across the head of Joe's cock.

"Never that." Joe tensed his legs, so he wouldn't fall. "Even in my dreams I could never imagine you on your knees in front of me. In my head it was always the other way around."

"I'll kneel for you any day of the week." Doc bent forward, and Joe instinctively locked his hips, so he wouldn't thrust. The suction, Doc's hands cradled around the rest of his exposed shaft. It was all too much and not enough. Looking down, Joe could see Doc's own cock, bright red on the tip and leaking like a sieve. He had to have a taste before he exploded. Pushing Doc away, although he cursed himself for being a madman for doing it, he bent down, lifting his mate under the armpits and setting him on the bed.

"I've never done this before," was all Joe had time to say before his tongue was searching out Doc's unique juices. Licking wasn't going to cut it, he was desperate for his first taste of cock – his mate's cock and as Joe stretched his lips around Doc's mushroomed head, his heart sang. He was so glad he waited because he knew no one could ever taste as good as his mate.

Doc leaned back, the gray skin of his abs rippling as he tensed and relaxed. Joe didn't have a clue what he was doing. All he knew was that suction felt amazing around his cock and teeth were a mood killer. He bobbed down, feeling his gag reflex kick in, but that was one of the many things he'd researched. He slurped back up, then bobbed down again, breathing through his nose. This time he was prepared for the gag feeling and breathed through it, pushing Doc's cock in his mouth that little bit further.

The moans falling from Doc's mouth, along with the gentle hand on his head was all the encouragement Joe needed. His head bobbed up and down in a soothing rhythm and it was easy to ignore the ache in his jaw. Doc's breathing got faster, and Joe could feel it – that electric moment that proceeded climax. Sucking faster, Joe was determined to pull every speck of spunk from his mate.

"Damn, mate," Doc said, and Joe didn't imagine the fondness in his voice. But as his mouth filled with his mate's release Joe savored the musky, bitter and definitely salty essence, feeling a beam of pride. He'd done that, reduced his mate to a hushed whisper and trembling limbs.

"Oh, babe, that was incredible." Doc pulled him up for another harsh kiss, but his flushed features were Joe's reward. Or so Joe thought. "I'm wearing a plug, if you want inside me," Doc whispered. "I was rather hoping we could have a midday fuck."

"You...?" Joe pulled back, he couldn't believe his ears. But Doc pulled his legs up to his chest, exposing his hole and Joe groaned. He knew what a butt plug was of course, but seeing the black silicone forcing Doc's hole open, laying flush against his pale skin brought a warmth to Joe's cheeks of an entirely different sort.

"How do I, can I just...?" Joe's fingers traced where silicone and skin met. He'd never seen anything so erotic in his life.

"This was in my coat pocket." Doc held out a single use sachet of lube.

"You put that on you, then gently ease that plug out. It's not the biggest one I've got but it flares wide inside. I wanted to be ready for you and knew we could be short of time during the day."

In his quietly methodical and almost clinical way, Doc had hidden depths. Joe hadn't even thought about having sex during the day with his mate, because he was worried about...too many things that weren't his mate. But as he coated his ready cock with lube and gently eased the black plug from his mate's ass, Joe vowed he'd do better. He'd learn all the things that Doc enjoyed and be a lot more thoughtful.

Sinking into Doc's willing hole was a fresh reminder of their claiming the night before. Unhooking Doc's legs from his hands, Joe wrapped them around his hips and leaned forward. Doc hurriedly grabbed a thin sheet and draped it over his abs. "Thank you," Joe said simply as he started to gently thrust. He wanted this to last – to savor being in the moment. "Thank you for thinking of things I didn't even know I needed. Thank you for caring and thinking about my comfort and thank you, thank you, thank you," he peppered the last thank yous with kisses, "For finally putting me out of misery."

"I freely admit I've been an old fool," Doc chuckled. "Now fuck me, stud, we only have an hour for lunch and I haven't eaten yet."

Considering Joe didn't think he'd last a minute with the heat of his mate's rectum squeezing on his cock just firm enough to drive him wild, he felt he made a good showing in lasting just under five minutes. As far as savoring the moment went, it was glorious. But as his balls ached and his body trembled all over with the force of his orgasm, Joe flicked a casual look at the plug laying near Doc's head.

"Swallow me down again, and I'll put that plug back in, so you'll know your seed is inside me all afternoon," Doc whispered, and Joe groaned before covering his mate's face with more kisses. It was easier than trying to say thank you with words. He didn't know if the caveman feelings he had rising in his chest and stirring his loin were from his animal or his human side, but the whole idea of his sperm being held inside his mate which any sensitive nose could smell made him want to beat his chest and howl to the moon. And no, it wasn't typical buffalo behavior but that didn't stop him easing his cock out of its tight home and bending his head to his mate's newly hardened erection.

/~/~/~/~/

Six o'clock couldn't come soon enough, and Doc had never been happier to hit the lock on his door. It didn't take long for word to spread around town that Joe was spending time in the office with his new mate.

186

Doc saw more patients in that one afternoon, than he'd seen in the whole of the previous week.

"I didn't realize you were always so busy," Joe said as Doc escorted him upstairs. "I wouldn't have thought there'd be too much for a doctor to do in a shifter town."

"Normally, there isn't a lot to do. Most shifters take care of themselves and I don't see them unless something is extremely painful or septic. Pregnancies are the bulk of my business, but not today," Doc grumped. "I've never seen so many trumped up injuries in my life than I did this afternoon. I mean did you see Liam's so-called wound? It was a damn splinter, for goodness sake."

"Liam was probably checking to make sure I was okay. He was the only one I told about you," Joe confessed. "I promise, it was none of that crying and true confessions stuff. He just guessed one day, and I couldn't lie but I told him not to say a word to anyone else."

"Water under the bridge, my mate." Doc kissed Joe's cheek. "Well, what do you think? It's not much, but I call it home." He hurried through to the kitchen to pull out another one of Mrs. Hooper's meals, leaving Joe to wander around. She'd been one of the afternoon visitors, increasing his ready-meal stockpile now he had someone else to look after. It was her way of saying congratulations and while Doc didn't think he'd escaped the lecture he could see brewing in her eyes, she'd left off verbally stripping him of his balls while Joe was around.

His apartment took up the entire top story of what was a huge house. Originally, it'd been configured into a number of small bedrooms, but when Doc bought the place, he knocked a lot of the walls out, creating wide open living spaces and an extra-large master suite for himself.

"This is amazing." Joe came to stand at the kitchen counter and looking out of the window. "You can see half the town from here."

"That's not always a good thing when Cam turfs out his drinkers at some ungodly hour." Doc put another bowl in the microwave. It smelled like a lamb dish of some sort. "But there was never any point in my having a house outside of town when I could get called in any time. Being here means anyone can knock on my door and know they'll get me."

"It will be sad giving up my little house." Joe leaned on the counter and Doc really shouldn't have noticed the way that pose showcased Joe's ass, but he couldn't help it. "But it would be pointless for us to have two houses, wouldn't it?"

Get your head out of his ass. Joe is looking for guidance here. "I don't see why you should get rid of it." Doc found the plates and cutlery needed and put them on the counter. Joe immediately picked them up and placed them on the table. "We could use it as a weekend home, sometimes, or when you have a few nights off. I can make up a sign for the door here, letting people know to call me if there's an emergency. It's not as though you live miles and miles out of town."

"You wouldn't mind?" Joe's face brightened. "I know it's not much, but it was the first place I could genuinely call my own. I don't owe anything on it, and I can easily pay the rates and taxes and still contribute here."

Doc's first instinct was to tell Joe he needn't pay anything at all. His house was owned outright and while Doc didn't make a lot of money as a doctor now, he used to when he worked in human hospitals. Canny investments meant they'd never have to work again if they didn't want to, but Doc knew Joe was a proud man, and a fair one. "I don't have a lot of expenses here," he said as the microwave dinged to let him know dinner was ready. "I pay the electricity and water, of course, as well as rates and taxes. My only other expense is food, and Mrs. Hooper gets most of that money."

"That does smell wonderful," Joe said as Doc set the bowl on the table. "I quite like cooking though. Do you think Mrs. Hooper would be mortally offended if we didn't have quite as many of her meals as you're used to?"

"Knowing Mrs. Hooper, she probably already knows." Doc laughed. "I swear that woman knows everything that goes on in town before it even happens. Once she sees you in store buying food, she'll be pushing her recipes onto you, claiming she knows the foods I prefer."

"Is she right?" Doc noticed Joe waited for him, before serving himself.

"Well, she makes a damn good stew," Doc said, digging into his. "But, the problem with readymade meals is that it means I never get the chance to eat a freshly grilled steak or enjoy a roast every now and then."

"I can cook those." Joe grinned. "There isn't much I won't eat although I didn't learn to cook until I moved into my own house and then it was all trial and error. I'm no Gordan Ramsey, but I can create a decent enough meal. It'd be nice to cook for someone else for a change."

Reminded again of how much time Joe spent alone, Doc couldn't help but ask. "What sorts of things do you do in your spare time? I know you're not one for going out socializing, but you can't work all the time, surely?"

"I renovated a lot," Joe said around a mouthful of stew. "My house was basically a shell when I bought it, but it was all I could afford. I've worked nights for years, usually because no one else wanted those shifts. When my Uncle Robert was in charge, the deputies were all lazy and on the take. Working nights was a great way of avoiding the shit in the office. With Rocky it's different. He offered me day shifts a while ago, but," he shrugged and flashed a quick grin at Doc. "At the time no one cared when I was working, so I just stuck with those shifts while Rocky and Mal investigated the Quincys and kept on top of the paperwork. I'll have a word to Mal about the roster tomorrow."

"Do we really get that much trouble here?" Doc was enjoying his stew, but he loved talking to Joe more.

"No, not really. That's why, even if I stay on the night shifts, most of the time I can be on call from home. There was more trouble when the Quincys were running the show because they never used to jail or banish anyone who were caught." Joe looked up and grimaced. "They were mostly Quincy family members. The crime rate, such as it was for

Arrowtown, dropped by more than seventy percent when they were kicked out of town."

"The Quincys did that much damage?" Doc couldn't believe it. The Quincys had ruled Arrowtown for decades to his knowledge and although he didn't keep tabs on the local gossip, he'd never heard of them causing too much trouble.

"They never did anything that couldn't be covered up or hushed up by paying out money. Vandalism, petty theft, that sort of thing. But yeah, Uncle Robert's sons were the worst. And we can't forget dear Uncle Myron, who might not have ever lived in town, but used this place as his base for a lot of his nefarious dealings. If I hadn't been told differently, I would have sworn it's Myron who actually wants this town back under the Quincy family control."

"I've never heard of him."

"You wouldn't have." Joe's dark eyes met his. "Every family has a black sheep, even buffalo shifters. Myron is the Quincy black sheep. He's run guns, drugs, and women. If there's an illegal gambling den in town, his name is on it. He doesn't understand the meaning of the word no. If money doesn't buy what he wants, then he takes it anyway, with force if necessary. But, he doesn't like to get his hands dirty which is why he's never been caught. The only decent thing Harold ever did was keep Myron out of the town limits."

Doc put down his knife and fork. Suddenly, the threat against Joe and the town sounded ominous. "If you're right, and I have no reason to think you're not, then this business with Harold and Robert is a lot more serious than them just having their nose put out of joint because they were banished. Has Rocky and Mal come up with any evidence there was money laundering or stuff being run through town that the public doesn't know about?"

"I don't know." Doc watched as Joe thought about it, but his mate shook his head. "Damn it, it's not likely they'd even know what to look for. Myron could have had his claws in this town for years and there's no saying what Harold and Robert might have covered up."

"Who's investigating the city books?"

"Simon, I think, but," Joe looked at the clock on the wall. "He's probably still down in the jail with Hargraves."

"We need to talk to them, now." Doc's animal was riding him hard and he'd learned a long time ago not to ignore him. A loud boom suddenly filled the night air, followed by the screeching of tires as a car drove off and Doc's heart sank as Joe leapt from his seat. *Or we could be too late.*

Chapter Twelve

As Joe ran down the street all he could see was a mass of rubble where the sheriff's office had been. Scanning the parking lot, his adrenaline went into overdrive when he saw Rocky and Mal's bikes knocked over in the parking lot. "Rocky. Mal," he yelled, his heart returning to normal rate when he saw the pair running over from Cam's.

"What the fuck?" Rocky's eyes were flashing wolf and not even Mal's hand on his arm held him back.

"Who was in there?" Joe said urgently. "Who was working tonight?"

"Liam, but he wasn't in the office. He's on call." Mal said turning to look down the road as a stream of bikes headed their way. "Looks like they got the message. I text Ra as soon as we heard the explosion."

"Fucking knocked the bottles from the bar," Cam grumbled but Joe could sense anger in him too. "Did anyone see the car that drove off?"

"Worry about that later," Mal shook his head. "Hargraves was inside that lot." He pointed to the rubble.

"Simon? Did Simon get out?" Joe didn't know the snake shifter very well, but he and Darwin's children were less than a year old.

"I'm here. I left that skuzz-ball in his cell over half an hour ago." Simon got off his bike and hurried over with Ra on his heels. Brutus was also there, scanning the crowd that had gathered, mostly from Cam's bar. Liam hurried to Rocky's side, with Trent, his mate shadowing him. "We're going to have to dig him out. It's not right to leave him buried under there."

"I'll shift and find him first, or at least roughly where he might be," Mal said stripping off his shirt. "There's no point in carting all this rubble for nothing."

"What the hell happened here?" Mrs. Hooper, hair tied up in a scarf and clutching her dressing gown around her ample form pushed through the crowd. "Is everyone safe?"

"Mrs. Hooper, why don't we move back and let these men work. I'm sure the mayor will make a statement shortly." Joe threw a thankful glance at Doc who was escorting Mrs. Hooper to a safe distance away. Mal was sniffing over the rubble and then for some reason, started moving away from the bomb site, over the car park to the road that ran behind Cam's bar. But he didn't stop there.

"I thought he was sniffing out that sleazy lawyer," Rocky said, scratching his head.

"I've got a horrible suspicion that's exactly what he's doing." Joe sprinted after Mal, Rocky hot on his heels. Mal circled once, looking toward the road, and then padded to the back of Cam's bar. There wasn't much there. An old chiller, a dumpster, and crates of empty bottles stacked up waiting to be picked up for recycling. Mal loped back and forth, his light fur bright under the security lights, sniffing at the dumpster and then the chiller and then the dumpster again.

"Is Hargraves hiding here?" Rocky whispered. Mal nodded. Rocky jerked his head to the chiller and Joe took the dumpster. *Gods, I get the glamorous jobs,* he thought as he swung the lid of the dumpster open as quietly as he can, making sure the lid didn't bang on the wall. Bags of trash interspersed with rotting food made Joe's eyes water, but there, in the corner, hidden by a large trash bag was a definite rustle of something bigger than a rat. At least Joe hoped it was Hargraves. He didn't want to be screaming like a girl in front of his boss if he found a furry four-footed rodent.

Creeping silently around to where he thought he saw movement, Joe wanted to hold his nose. Moldy potatoes fought for ranking stench rights with something that resembled rotting socks. Playing a hunch, he lightly scratched on a bag close to where he though Hargraves might be hiding. Sure enough, he was rewarded with a tiny whisper. "Myron, is that you? Thank god you came back for me...." Hargraves snapped his mouth shut as Joe whipped out the bag covering the lawyer with one hand and grabbed him around the back of the neck with the other.

"No. No. You're not locking me up again." Hargraves struggled, fishing in his pants for something. A loud bang, a sharp pain and Rocky's growl was the last thing Joe remembered before he hit the dirt.

/~/~/~/~/

Doc's head snapped up as he heard the gunshot and he was running towards the sound before his brain realized what his feet were doing. *Please, please, please, please,* but his animal half already knew what his mind was dreading. Rounding the corner of Cam's bar, Doc's worst nightmare came to life. Rocky was strangling Hargraves with both hands while Mal was begging Rocky to stand down, that Hargraves had information they needed. But it was Joe who commanded Doc's attention. His body starkly highlighted by the harsh security lights, blood darkening his blue shirt, Joe's eyes were closed, and he was completely motionless.

"I'll kill him," Doc snarled. "Fucking get out of my way, Rocky. I'm going to fucking kill that useless lawyer and shit on his corpse."

"Tend to your mate." Simon was there, and Ra too, with Brutus providing back up. Their brute strength and big frames effectively blocking Hargraves from Doc's sight. He wanted to push past; he wanted to tear Hargraves limb from limb, but then Joe moaned, and Doc was there in an instant, his professionalism pushing away his need for revenge.

"I need my bag," he yelled, ripping Joe's shirt from neck to hem. "Lights. More lights. I don't dare move him."

"Should he shift, Doc?" Liam's face was white as he knelt on Joe's other side.

"The bullet has gone too close to the heart. A shift could kill him." Doc probed around the wound, one hand sliding around Joe's back. As he suspected, no exit wound. *Come on, babe, don't give up on me now.* He knew some shifters had mind links, but his mating was still new, and he hadn't given it a try. But now, with Joe's pulse erratic and his breathing shallow, Doc was prepared to dance naked down the Main Street with flowers in his hair if it helped his mate in any way. *I haven't told you I love you, yet. I've got huge plans for our anniversary. We have a wedding to plan. Don't you dare give up on us now.*

"Where's my damn bag?" Every second counted. He looked up, seeing a mass of concerned faces, but no bag in sight.

"Here, Doc." Cam was there with Trent and someone who looked like his brother. "We brought the top of the bed in case that would help and lights. Tell us where you want them."

"I need to see." Doc's hand was shaking, and he slapped it on his knee, so the tremors wouldn't show. "Whoever's tallest, stand holding the light above Joe's head. Anyone else, stand in a semi-circle around that one, holding them as high as you can. Stay on this side of me. Liam grab that sheet, fold it and slide it carefully under my mate's head. Leave the bed for now, I need to get this bullet out first." *Come on training, don't desert me now.*

In his almost four centuries of living, Doc had removed hundreds of bullets from shattered bodies. The one lodged in Joe was only a small caliber, likely from a hand gun, yet the size had allowed the bullet to pass through his mate's ribs. Blood was flowing steadily under his fingers and Doc prayed to the Fates, Gods, and anyone who would listen that the bullet hadn't nicked an artery.

Scrambling through his bag, Doc pulled out a long thin pair of tweezers with a magnetic end. "Hold that light steady," he ordered as he carefully pushed the metal through Joe's skin. Stopping with barely an inch inside, Doc had to control himself, his hands were trembling so much. Fortifying himself with a long glance at his mate's pale face, his blond hair a stark contrast to the pavement, Doc gave himself a sound talking to. *You can do this. You've trained for decades for just this moment. Ignore the blood. It's just a small insignificant little bullet. Just put the probe in and pull it out again slow and steady.*

It seemed like hours, but in reality, it was not even a minute before Doc was holding the tweezers upright, a small mashed bit of metal clinging to the end of them.

"I'll need that, Doc." Rocky stepped forward with a plastic evidence bag. Doc dropped the bullet in it and then turned back to his patient – his mate. At least this was a clean wound. There wasn't a hint of poison or anything coming from the bullet entry site. Grabbing some sterile gauze, Doc taped it over the hole and then let his hand linger on Joe's head. His mate's color was coming back into his face, and the gauze on his chest stayed white meaning the blood flow had slowed. Doc would put a few stitches in it, but not while Joe was on the pavement. Lethargy flooded his muscles as his adrenalin subsided.

"Doc, are you okay?" Liam asked. "Do you want a hand getting him on the bed, so we can carry him back to the surgery?"

As much as Doc would rather do it himself, Joe needed to remain flat until the stitches were in and he'd regained consciousness. "Yes, boys, if you wouldn't mind. Liam, can you take his feet?" Doc slipped his hands under Joe's broad shoulders. Cam and Trent held the bed base steady, sliding it under Joe's body as Doc and Liam lifted him.

"We'll all take a corner," Rocky appeared, his voice grim. "Simon and Brutus have taken the person responsible for this back to the mayor's office for interrogation."

"I want him dead," Doc hissed as a somber procession made their way to Doc's office. "I know he's human, but this is a shifter affair. He came into a shifter town, claiming to work for other shifters so he's subject to our laws. I know he's got information you need, and now I know Joe'll be okay, I can live with that. But I want your solemn word, when you've wrung him dry I want him dead."

Rocky didn't answer, probably because he was still wearing his sheriff's uniform, but from the growls coming from Trent, Cam, and Liam, Doc was reasonably confident Hargraves wouldn't be leaving Arrowtown alive.

Chapter Thirteen

"Gods, this is getting to be a habit." Joe rubbed the ache in his chest, his fingers finding gauze. "Doc?" The surgery was dark, the only light coming through the door from the waiting room.

"I'm here, babe. I haven't left your side and I thought I told you to call me Nathan." Doc loomed over the bed. "How are you feeling?"

"Like I got shot." Joe reached for Doc's hand. "The Fates knew what they were doing when they paired me with you, Nathan," he stressed his mate's name deliberately. "Although, I feel weird calling you that when we're in your office."

"I'm not sure if my heart can take much more of seeing you in here like this either," Doc teased softly, but in the half-light Joe could see his mate's usually immaculate hair looked as though he'd spent hours running his fingers through it and there were dark circles under his eyes. Joe wanted to hold his mate close and never let him go, but the events of the evening flooded his brain.

"Did they find out how Hargraves got out of the cell? Does he know who blew it up? Was anyone else hurt?"

"Rocky and Ra will be around in the morning with an update. Everything is under control," Doc soothed. "I'm more concerned about you. Do you need to shift?"

Looking down at his chest, Joe nodded. "I don't usually shift in town. Do you have somewhere handy that you go when your animal wants to stretch his legs?"

"Nowhere fancy, I'm afraid." Doc's fingers plucked at the covers. "I've set up the basement for when I want to shift. That way, I can be sure no one can see or hear me."

"That's a clever idea." Joe smiled. He could smell Doc's embarrassment and that was the last thing his mate should be feeling when he'd clearly been through an emotional time. "Can you stand upright in the basement when you're on two legs? Is there room for my massive bulk to stand and lie down with you?"

"It's not comfortable. It hasn't got any grass, but it is big enough, yes. It's the same square footage as our apartment."

"Our apartment." Joe's smile got wider. "I love the way you say that." Pushing on the bed, he sat up, a small head rush making him feel woozy for a second, but it passed quickly. "I know you're worried for me, babe, but I promise it takes more than a single bullet to take a buffalo down." He reached over, pulling Doc against his chest, feeling the tremble in his mate's limbs. "I promise I'll be fine."

"You can't promise that." Doc spoke so low it was hard to hear him. "I visited my worst nightmare this evening...."

"And you came through it and so did I and what doesn't kill us, makes us stronger, right? Babe, I can't imagine how hard that must have been, but you're the one who pulled me through it. Damn, I didn't even feel the bullet when it hit me, let alone anything else."

"There was so much blood." Doc's eyes were closed. Joe loosened the leather tie in his hair, so he could stroke his fingers through it. There really wasn't anything he could say. He couldn't offer to give up his job or anything else romantic because he really didn't know how to do anything else. But he could comfort his mate when Doc needed him to, and considering what the pair had been through, that was a miracle in itself.

"Come on," Joe said at last, moving Doc far enough away so he could swing his legs around, without letting go of him. "I can feel your lovely Komodo shuffling under your skin. He needs to know I'm all right as well.

Let's go and shift and then maybe get a shower and some sleep?"

"You won't be repulsed, you know, with the way I look when I'm shifted?" Doc lifted his head, his face a lot more relaxed and Joe knew his scent had worked wonders. He wasn't sure where his mate's insecurities were coming from, but he hastened to reassure him.

"I've only seen natural Komodo dragons on video, but they've always impressed me with their strength. You have to remember, I'm not a pretty animal either, what with my woolly head and long rangy body. At least you don't have skinny legs."

That got a chuckle out of his mate and that's exactly what Joe was going for. "Any chance I can get a kiss out of you before we head downstairs? I guess I need to know I'm still attractive to you, even with a hole in my chest."

"Don't remind me," Doc groaned, banging his head lightly on Joe's shoulder. "Actually, do remind me, otherwise I'm likely to forget this bed is damned uncomfortable and claim your ass, chest wound or not."

"Hmm, I can get on board with that. Definitely later," Joe promised, sticking out his lips. He wasn't sure, because the mental and emotional aspects of reptiles was something scientists could only guess at. But he did wonder if a lot of his mate's angst came from the fact they weren't double claimed. Joe intended to change all that in the very near future. In fact, he was looking forward to it. In the meantime, Doc's hands in his hair sent shivers down his spine, and Doc's kiss promised his claiming would be something he would always remember.

/~/~/~/~/

Doc kept up a steady litany in his head as he helped Joe down the stairs to the basement under the office. *My drool is not toxic. There's no reason for my animal form to bite my mate and release any venom. I won't hurt him or see him as a threat or a food source. If Ra doesn't eat that little bunny of his in his tiger form, and Simon is happy for Darwin's tiny mouse form to run all over his scales, then my animal isn't going to take a chunk out of Joe.*

It didn't help Doc's nerves much, but Joe's delight at the little additions he'd made to the basement was worth seeing. "This is incredible." Joe said, looking around, his eyes bright. "You did all this yourself?"

'All this', was the pile of rocks Doc had in one corner of the large space, a heat lamp situated over an elevated flat rock big enough to take his shifted form. In another corner, there was a small pond, wide enough for him to walk into so he could drink, the water kept fresh and cool thanks to a small pump that ran all the time. The floor around the pool was covered in a foot thick of sand and in the third corner was a large palm, growing in a pot, it's leaves gaining the sunlight it needed with the help of lamps and a small one-way tinted window that sat behind it.

The room was hot, just the way Doc's animal liked it and now he could see it had an added benefit when Joe stripped off his clothes. "I could sunbathe in here in the middle of winter," he said happily. "Did you want me to shift first, or will it be easier for you, if I stay in my human form until your animal is used to me?"

"I think I need verbal feedback," Doc said, pulling off his shirt. Getting naked was never a problem, not around Joe whose gaze heated as Doc dropped his pants. "But please stand still. I'm…." Doc had a chronic problem with admitting a weakness, but he pushed himself to be honest with his mate. "I'm not sure how this will go and that worries me."

"I'm not worried," Joe said cheerfully. "You're fully cognizant in your shifted form. You've cared about me for years…yes, I do realize that now, so take that look off your face. Please shift. It's a bit like sex. Always better after the first time."

Wishing he had Joe's confidence, Doc called on his animal form. Unlike furry shifters who landed on four feet in the blink of an eye, his shifting process was more gradual. The leathery skin on his torso took on scales, before spreading over his whole body. His face lengthened and rounded at the end and his arms and legs bent at the elbows and knees as the Komodo came forward. His tail morphed from the base of his spine, it's thickness and strength strong enough to hold him upright. Doc opened his mouth as his animal took over, scenting the air with his long forked tongue. He dropped to the floor, instantly aware he wasn't alone.

/~/~/~/~/

Joe was fascinated, watching his mate shift. In most shifts he'd seen, the process was too fast to watch, but the Komodo dragon emerged slowly, taking almost a full minute to come through. The deputy side of his brain and the part of him that automatically worried about his mate, was concerned, thinking that Doc trying to shift when under attack would leave him vulnerable during that time. But there was no disputing he'd be more than capable of protecting himself once he was fully shifted.

"Wow. Just wow." As Doc instructed, Joe stood perfectly still. The intensity of the dragon's eyes and the way his tongue flicked out caused his fingers to twitch. He had an irrational urge to cover his cock and balls. Doc's tongue was more than a foot long in this form which set Joe's mind off in directions he'd never thought possible.

Moving slowly, as if the animal was afraid of him, Doc got steadily closer. Each foot was deliberately placed on the floor, the dragon's huge body and tail swaying with every step. As he got closer, Joe could appreciate the shine of lights on the animal's scales; there was a certain elegant power emanating from Doc's form. Joe was fascinated, and completely entranced.

"I've never seen such a serious looking animal form before," he said with a bit of a chuckle, because Doc was intense. "Strangely sexy, but yep, my mind isn't going there," because with the shift, Doc's scent was stronger, and Joe was newly mated. His cock reacted predictably, something he did his best to ignore.

"Is it okay to touch?" He held out his hand, much like he would with a reluctant pet. Doc's tongue flickered closer, but didn't touch him, but he slowly moved his body around and rubbed his neck against Joe's palm.

Petting the scales, which Joe found surprisingly warm, all he could think was the experience was so rare and so amazing. That his mate could shift into such an intriguing reptile was something out of a dream for Joe. He loved his animal form and respected his animal spirit, but Doc took the form of a creature from ancient history, and even though his hands told him what he was doing, Joe's mind could barely comprehend he was touching a Komodo dragon. His Komodo dragon.

The heat from the lamps warmed Joe's skin and he lost track of time as he stroked over Doc's scales. All he could think was how lucky he was. The two years of heart ache when Doc wouldn't acknowledge him; his harsh words. None of it meant anything anymore. Doc had trusted him with his deepest secret and Joe felt honored and awed. It took a sharp nudge from Doc's snub nose, to remind Joe it was actually him that was meant to shift.

"You're amazing," Joe said, stepping back to give himself plenty of room to shift. "Watch that tail of yours around my legs." He smiled to show he was teasing and let his shift flow over him.

Joe was tall in both forms, so his perspective on life didn't change much when he was standing on four legs. His animal was keen to sniff though, and Doc stood patiently as Joe's nose took in the long body, the thick tail and then came back up and snorted on Doc's neck. That made the Komodo move, scampering away with surprising speed to the pool where he scooped up water and tilted his head back enabling him to swallow. The buffalo flicked his tail lazily. He didn't really care that his new friend felt the need to run off. He snuffled at the palm tree and scratched the top of his head against the rough bark.

After quenching his thirst, Doc ambled over and climbed up the rocks, splaying himself out on the flat one, watching the buffalo explore. When Joe realized there was nothing for him to eat in the room, he plodded over to the side of the flat rock, and rested against the edge, happy to just be with his mate. As far as first meetings in shifted form went, Joe felt it was a huge success. Although that didn't stop him daydreaming about running with Doc in the woods behind his own home. *Maybe one day.*

Chapter Fourteen

Doc cursed as he woke to the sound of someone pounding on his front door. A quick check of the clock showed it wasn't quite eight in the morning. "Someone had better be dying," he yelled as he grabbed his robe off the back of the door and stumbled down the stairs to his surgery. Flinging open the door, he scowled as he saw Rocky and Mal. "You woke me up and you're not bleeding," he snarled.

"But we brought coffee and breakfast from the diner." Mal held up his offerings.

"Fine. Come on upstairs. Let me put some clothes on and wake Joe."

"Don't dress on our account, Doc," Rocky teased. "I'm sure you've got nothing we haven't seen before."

"That's what you think." Doc snapped his mouth shut and led the way back upstairs. Joe met them at the top, scratching his bed-mussed hair, a pair of jeans slung low on his hips. There wasn't a scratch on his bare chest.

"Hey guys. I was going to find you at the mayor's office today. What's happening?"

Leaving them in the kitchen to dish out breakfast, Doc hurried through the bedroom and threw on the first pants and top he could find. Since shifting the night before, his hair wasn't tied up and was a mass of tangles. Doc impatiently tugged his brush through it, his eyes searching for a leather tie. He could hear snatches of the conversation, but not enough to make out what everyone was saying. At the moment, it seemed like Mal was checking that Joe was okay, but then Joe gave a small cry of distress and Doc abandoned his hair and ran back to where he'd left them. "Babe, what's wrong?"

"They want to suspend me from my job." There were genuine tears in

Joe's eyes and Doc turned on Rocky, his teeth bared.

"What the hell did my mate do wrong? He was nowhere near the office when it blew up. He apprehended Hargraves. It wasn't his fault he got shot. What's that piece of shit been saying now?"

"What our hot-headed sheriff meant to say," Mal said calmly, shooting a warning look at Rocky, "was that we thought it might be a good idea to give the impression you've been suspended. Joe is not now, nor has he ever been under suspicion for anything. But," Mal sighed. "There's no easy way to say this – Joe, you're a target. A great big one, if anything Hargraves said can be believed."

"You guys can scent lies," Doc nudged Joe into the nearest chair, reaching over to get his coffee. "Either he's telling the truth or he's not."

"None of us smelled any deceit." Rocky started dishing out the breakfast boxes they'd brought with them. "For what it's worth, I don't think Hargraves meant to shoot anyone, let alone an officer of the law. He was sobbing like a baby while Simon and Brutus were holding him and as soon as he saw me and Mal he started blubbering all over again."

"Like I give a shit about him." Doc stabbed into his potato cake with his fork. "What's all this about Joe being a target?"

"That's the only thing we got out of this mess that made sense," Mal said. "The Quincy's are behind this, we know that. For whatever reason, they want Joe dead for being a traitor to the family name."

"That could be for a lot of reasons," Joe said. Doc noticed he wasn't eating, but he was hanging onto his coffee cup like a lifeline, his eyes still damp. "I have never involved myself in any of the family crimes, I'm the only Quincy in town who would stand up to them, and I've mated a man. Quincys don't approve of any of that."

"The thing is," Rocky leaned over the table, "How the hell do they know this stuff? Yes, Hargraves saw you two together at the diner and you said you were mates then, but he hasn't had a chance to get in touch with anyone else. Doc, you didn't tell Harold, did you?"

"No, I let him assume I was visiting Joe in a professional capacity."

"A professional capacity that cost me twenty bucks." Rocky winced as Mal elbowed him in the ribs. "Sorry, I am happy for you both, but you see what I am getting at. Hargraves didn't seem surprised to see you in the diner, Joe. But Harold thought you were on death's door and he's always been a wimp. There's no way he'd instigate something like blowing up the sheriff's office. Robert is dead, so who does that leave?"

"Didn't Hargraves tell you?" Doc swallowed down the last of his potato and shoved his fork in some bacon. One of the joys of being the type of shifter he was. Komodo dragons could eat through any situation.

"Humans let Hargraves out of his cell," Rocky said around a mouthful of food. "They broke down the back door, unlocked his cell. The keys are always hanging on a hook by the door, in case of an emergency. Some guy in a balaclava shoved the gun in Hargraves hand and told him to keep quiet and run. They said some guy called Myron would be back for him and then took off."

Joe put down his fork. "Doc and I were just talking about finding you, to chat about Myron when we heard the explosion."

"Well, that's one point for our team. You know who he is." Rocky shoved a forkful of bacon and eggs into his mouth. He waved the now empty fork at Joe to continue.

"Myron is Harold's older brother, another uncle of mine," Joe said slowly. "You won't have heard about him before, because one of Harold and Robert's main jobs was keeping him out of the public eye and away from law enforcement. He runs his own criminal enterprise but not in shifter towns. Well, not Arrowtown. Harold insisted, right from the start, and this is just secondhand you understand, but Harold said he couldn't keep his mayor job if Myron lived in town. We all agree Robert was a crook too, but he'd have been drummed out of his position years ago if Myron had been in town. Myron's not a petty criminal, like Robert's sons."

"Fucking brilliant." Rocky scraped his plate and then pushed it away. "So, we have a criminal mastermind, who may or may not have had ties to this town, who for some unknown reason wants the status quo restored which is why my office got blown up and why you're walking around with a target on your back. Have I grasped the situation so far?"

"Joe doesn't know anything more about Myron than what he's telling you." Doc hated the look of defeat on his mate's face. "We were coming to tell you about it because we thought it had to do with money; maybe funds being laundered through the city books or something. We didn't know what the tie might have been exactly but would have warned you if we'd had the chance. It's my mate that's in danger here. You notice whoever's been watching us made sure the only person in jail was Hargraves. Simon had barely been gone thirty minutes when it blew, and you can't tell me that's coincidence."

"And they let him out, so they weren't told to kill anyone, except our deputy Joe," Mal agreed. "But if Joe was the target, why let Hargraves out? Why not just let him get caught in the blast?"

"The only reason Myron would keep Hargraves alive is because he's useful. That might tie into the money angle too." Joe had abandoned his empty coffee cup and was nibbling on a piece of bacon. "I don't know a lot about Myron. I've only met him a couple of times my whole life, and I haven't seen him for years. But my cousins, Robert's sons, really looked up to him. I think a lot of the stuff they did was because they were hoping to catch Myron's eye and be taken into the family business."

"Shades of the godfather," Mal shook his head. "Okay. We can't touch Robert's sons unless they come to town, because they're banned from here. The humans that blew up the sheriff's office – same problem. I talked to the council last night, as did Ra. They are sending their liaison officer to pick up Hargraves and hand him over to the human authorities."

"What are they charging him with?" Joe asked. "I mean, we know he's up to his neck in shit, but human laws work differently to ours."

"I thought I had your word, Rocky." Doc glared at the alpha. "If Hargraves leaves here, Myron will get him out and in the meantime there's no way of knowing how much information he's picked up about us and this town since he's been here. Shifter justice demands I have the right to kill him for shooting my mate. A town meeting will bring the same verdict – you know it would."

Rocky bit his lip, casting a worried look at Mal who shook his head. "I can't let you do it, Doc," Rocky said at last. "I know, I know you have every right, but Joe's fine and…and…."

"Spit it out, Rocky," Joe said calmly, picking up another piece of bacon which must have been cold by now. "Things must be bad if you're going against shifter law."

"This doesn't leave this room, okay?" Rocky waited until they all nodded before continuing. "I think, and by me, I mean the guys at Ra's house, all think that there's more to this than anyone is seeing, and the council aren't being helpful. They see it as a town issue and nothing for them to worry about. I had to tell them about Hargraves. That's standard procedure when a human is involved in shifter issues."

"Why tell the council about it now? Why not just keep Hargraves here until Myron comes for him again?" Joe asked.

"Because too many people know he's here, and if someone else reported it to the council, we'd all be in the shit," Mal said. "It's clear there's a Quincy snitch in town. You said yourself, why was the sheriff's office empty when it was blown up? How did Hargraves and by extension, Myron, know you were still alive after Robert was killed? There's still too many things we don't know, and in the meantime, someone is watching us."

"But surely, that's all the more reason to keep Hargraves here?" Doc couldn't work out what Rocky and Mal were thinking. "If people know he's been sent off, to so-called human authorities, it undermines the shifter laws in this town. A lot of people care about Joe. They know he was shot by Hargraves. The only reason he's still alive now is because I had to dig a bullet out of my mate's chest before I could separate his worthless head from his body." Doc could feel his breathing quicken up and his heart was pounding so loud everyone would be able to hear it. All he could see in his mind's eye was his mate sprawled on the pavement with blood all over his chest. Joe grabbed his hand, he didn't even realize it was fisted, and squeezed it tight.

"We're hoping Hargraves will lead us to this Myron person," Mal said. "Face it, when it's all said and done,

Hargraves is a pawn. Yes, he knew about the crap coating Robert's horns, and yes, he did shoot Joe, but he wasn't lying when he said he didn't mean to. Shifter laws apply, yes, but that's one of the stupid aspects of the legal system. Those laws don't apply to Hargraves and because of those same laws, we can't go riding out to the farm Harold claims they are holed up in, with guns blazing. They are living outside of town limits."

"So, what's the point of tracking Hargraves out of town, then?" Joe asked, and Doc couldn't believe how calmly his mate was taking all this. His blood was boiling, and he was ready to go and find Hargraves and kill him now before he could cause any more trouble.

"We think Myron is in town," Rocky said. "Admittedly, we didn't know he was related to you when we were talking about it last night, but there is someone in town, a shifter, who is loyal to him, and knowing the family connection that now makes sense. The car carrying the people responsible for releasing Hargraves and bombing the office barely stopped in town. Cameras picked them up on one side of town, they drove straight through, stopped behind the cells, let Hargraves go, threw their bomb and left."

"Shifter towns aren't included in GPS systems, so the men had to have got instructions from somewhere," Joe mused, "otherwise how would they know where the sheriff office was? Someone in town must have seen me take Hargraves to the office yesterday morning and whoever was watching, knew he didn't leave."

"Simon was also tracked otherwise they wouldn't have let him go home first. Everyone in town knows he's a lawyer and newly mated, suggesting our watcher has got some heart," Mal agreed. "It's also common knowledge

Rocky and I get dinner at Cam's if we're working late."

"Humans wouldn't want to take on a shifter in a fight," Doc calmed down enough to contribute something to the conversation, albeit tersely. "Is it possible Myron didn't know the guys he hired very well, and was worried they'd be caught and questioned if someone else was in the office when they broke Hargraves out?"

"From what I understand, and please, I don't know this as fact," Joe said slowly, "Myron only has one or two people he trusts more than others. His trusted friends are not likely to be human. But my cousins used to brag all the time about Myron's huge network, about how he used to pay people off for information and how the 'little guys', their words not mine, never knew who the big boss was."

"If that's the case, good call on not wasting resources chasing that car. Those guys were probably paid to do a job by a middle man. Myron might not even know who they were exactly." Rocky nodded at Mal.

"That would also explain why Hargraves wasn't taken with them, especially if Myron was planning on using Hargraves for something else further down the track. I'm almost certain that's the only reason he's still alive," Joe said. "Did you ask Hargraves if he knew who Myron is?"

"He said he'd not heard that name before his rescuers mentioned it." Mal's quirked brow suggested he thought the lawyer had been evasive.

Leaning back in his chair, Joe took Doc's hand with him and Doc got a chance to see another side of his mate. He didn't just dive in with wild ideas, he didn't brag or try to upstage his friends in any way. He listened, and it was clear he was thinking all the time. "Let's assume," Joe said slowly, "that Harold doesn't know I recovered from Robert's attack. I think Myron, and Robert too, were keeping Harold in the dark. When

Harold told Doc about the possible raid in town, he said it was what he'd heard, but he didn't spill any significant details."

"That makes sense," Doc scoffed. "Harold couldn't fight his way out of a paper bag, and spending all those years as Mayor – shit, all he cared about was getting his dick serviced and counting his money."

"And the crux of his phone call was getting his job back as mayor," Joe reminded him. "He knew about the spell stuff on Robert's horns, but I doubt he could've applied it. Someone else had to be on or near the Forest farm that night."

"We thought it might have been Myron," Rocky said, but Joe shook his head.

"No. Myron is the type to ride in after the guns have stopped firing. Think. Think." Joe tapped his head with his free hand. "Dash. Dash is the connecting link."

"The deer shifter? Really?" Doc couldn't see what the link was.

"My cousins, Al and Wall used to run with the two older Dash boys. This was before you guys came here," Joe said to Rocky and Mal. "Dash's farm meets Forest's land on the western edge. Mr. Dash was sitting with Hargraves when you and I went to the diner for breakfast, babe. It all makes sense."

"That's right," Doc said as he thought back to that morning. "Hargraves was rude to Dash back then, but with everything else that happened, I didn't think anything of it at the time. The way Hargraves spoke to him suggested they knew each other."

"No one with the name of Dash has been in trouble since we took office," Rocky said. "I would've remembered the name if they had."

"No, the boys were never in trouble as such," Joe said quickly. "They came close to being jailed a couple of times. I remember there was an incident with a stolen car, but as Wall was the instigator and Robert paid the damages, the case never came to light. But I do think a visit to their farm is in order. I'll get dressed and call out there."

"Joe, you can't go," Mal said gently. "You're on suspension, remember?"

"No, I'm not. You suggested suspension because you're trying to protect me, and I appreciate it, I do." Joe's jaw firmed. "But, it won't do any good. If I'm a target, like you say, then I need to be doing my job. Hiding out here, or at my house, just makes it easier for people to get to me. What if Doc's surgery is bombed next with innocent people inside? Or if I'm out at my place, our weekend place," Doc was warmed by Joe's quick smile, "and someone decides to burn it down, or shoot me out there. Don't you see? This is my family doing this. I need to be a part of what happens next and not just as the target."

"The family side of things could make things awkward for you," Mal said hesitantly, looking at Rocky.

"Do you trust me?"

"Always, Joe. I see you as part of my family." Rocky met Joe's eyes.

"Then let me do this. Let me go and see the Dash's at least."

"We could go and have another talk to Hargraves before the council liaison guy gets here," Mal said. "If he thinks he's going to get used for something illegal, he might be more forthcoming when we tell him about Myron."

Doc spoke up before he thought about what he was saying. "I could give you a good excuse to get into the Dash household, Joe, if you didn't want to start questioning people right away. Rosie Dash broke her arm just a few days ago. I don't make house calls as a rule, but I could always say I was in the area because you were following up on Robert's death at the Forest farm."

"Are you looking to be deputized too, Doc?" Rocky relaxed back in his chair with a lazy grin.

If that's what it takes to protect my mate, Doc thought as he shrugged off the question. One thing was solid in his mind though. Until Myron, or whoever was doing this was caught, he wasn't letting his mate out of his sight and Rocky and Mal and even the mayor himself could all go to hell if they thought they could stop him.

Chapter Fifteen

It wasn't far to the Dash farm and Joe made it in good time. But he'd been worried about his mate, who'd been quiet since Rocky and Mal left to question Hargraves again. Trundling slowly down the dirt driveway that was a mass of pot holes, he risked a quick look at Doc's profile. "Are you okay," he asked quietly. "You're not still pissed at Rocky and Mal for trying to suspend me, are you?"

"No, babe, nothing like that." Doc's smile was quick but genuine. He rubbed his stomach. "Something we ate for breakfast disagreed with me and that doesn't happen very often in breeds like mine. I've just got an upset stomach, that's all."

Joe frowned. It wasn't common for shifters to get sick. "Would you rather sit in the car while I talk to the Dash's. I could just say I am making routine inquiries. Ask them if they saw or heard anything weird the night Robert was killed."

"A grumbly tummy is not going to stop me going in there with you," Doc said firmly. "Mrs. Dash is a lovely lady, even if she is a little harassed raising seven children. Little Rosie was a surprise. Her boys are all fourteen to twenty years older."

"See, that's why you're the perfect mate for me." Joe parked in front of the tired looking house and pecked Doc on the cheek. "I know the names of everyone in town, but you're the one who sees behind the scenes if you know what I mean."

"I see them when they're sick and often at their worst. It's not unlike what you do."

"Yeah, I've seen a lot of them at their worst," Joe laughed. Despite the threat against him, he was in uniform, doing the job he loved. Better yet, he had his protective mate by his side. "I see someone is peeking out of the window at us. We'd better go in."

"That'll be Rosie. She doesn't miss much, that little one."

Joe noticed Doc seemed a bit stiff getting out of the car, but he didn't say anything. A quick glance around the yard didn't reveal anything unusual. The old barn at the side of the house needed a lick of paint, and there were a few broken railings on the porch in front of the house. No one seemed to be around, but then it was close to lunchtime, so the family was probably in the house.

"Doc." It seemed little Rosie couldn't wait for them to get to the house and had opened the front door. "Did you come to see my arm? I've been doing what you said. I haven't lifted anything heavier than my dinner plate." She waved her bright pink cast as if to show it was still in good condition. Someone had drawn a purple unicorn on it, which Joe thought was really sweet.

"I was in the area and thought I would drop in and say hello." Joe loved to see the smile on Doc's face. "And see, I brought my mate, Deputy Joe with me too."

"I heard you got hurt too." Rosie's cute little face showed her concern. "Did the Doc give you a pretty pink cast like mine?"

"No, sadly not." Joe sighed and then winked as he smiled. "I didn't need a cast, but yours is very pretty. Is your Mom and Dad home? We'd like to say hello if they're around."

"Dad went out with Roe and Carmine, but Mom's here." Rosie grinned, showing she'd lost her two front baby teeth. "Come on, she's in the kitchen."

"Rosie, what have I told you about opening the front door?" It seemed Mrs. Dash wasn't in the kitchen.

"But they's not strangers, Mommy, they're the Doc and Deputy Joe all smart in his uniform."

"Thank you, Miss Rosie." Joe smiled at the flustered Mrs. Dash. "I hope we're not bothering you, Ma'am. I'm sure you've heard the news. The Doc and I are newly mated, and he decided to come with me on my rounds today. We were in the area and Doc told me about Rosie's arm, so we thought we'd come and say hello."

Joe was counting on Arrowtown hospitality and sure enough, Mrs. Dash smiled and indicated with her head back into the house. "If you can excuse the mess, you're welcome to come in and have a cup of coffee. Brian headed out with the two older boys early this morning. Said something about fixing up the old barn on the back of our place. The other boys have gone riding. I'm expecting them back at any time for lunch."

"We won't hold you up long," Doc said smoothly, "but a cup of coffee would be lovely. I didn't realize a deputy's work could be so time consuming. After you."

Joe loved Doc's courtly manners, and followed the two into the house, Rosie bouncing by his side. As Doc and Mrs. Dash went through the living room into the kitchen, Rosie tugged on Joe's pants and put her finger to her lips. "I'm just showing Deputy Joe my new doll house, Mommy," she said loudly, tugging Joe down a long hall.

"Make sure you're not being a nuisance, Rosie." Mrs. Dash's voice had that tone Joe had heard a thousand times before. It was that voice mothers used to be polite, but honestly, they were grateful for a five minute reprieve. Trusting Doc to keep Mrs. Dash occupied, Joe followed the little girl into what was obviously a well-loved room. There were explosions of pink everywhere.

"You have a lovely room, Miss Rosie," Joe said, looking around. It was a lovely room and Joe smiled, thinking while Rosie's arrival might not have been planned, having a wee girl after six boys gave the mother a chance to splash out on the pretty things she'd probably longed for, for years.

"I needs to talk to you," Rosie whispered loudly. "Your job is to catch bad people, right?"

Joe nodded.

"What happens to those bad people when you catches them?"

"That all depends." Joe kneeled down so he was eye level with the little girl. "You know about laws, right?"

It was Rosie's turn to nod.

"Well, then you know sometimes when bad people do bad things, and break those laws, they have to be punished, right?"

"Like when Jimmy broke my bestest doll and Daddy made him do work so he could buy me a new one."

"That's right. That's called restitution." Joe smiled. "Paying back someone who has had something taken from them."

Rosie looked towards the door and then crept closer. "But what if someone did something really bad. Worse than smashing down my new doll house bad."

Joe felt the hairs on the back of his neck stick up. "It would really depend on what that something was, Miss Rosie, and why the person did that bad thing. Sometimes good people do bad things for good reasons, and sometimes bad people make good people do bad things even if they don't want to. Do you see what I mean?"

Rosie nodded, her eyes widening as she heard her mother calling her. "I think you need to get out to the old barn. You might find some bad people. I don't like them here," she whispered, "but remember, my daddy is one of the good people."

Running out of the room, Rosie left Joe to follow at his own pace. It wasn't ethical to question the little girl. She wasn't a suspect. Chances are she overheard something not meant for little ears. It didn't help that Mrs. Dash kept flicking guilty glances at him when she thought he wasn't paying attention. Doc had barely finished his coffee when Joe stood up. "As you probably guessed, the sheriff's department is still investigating Robert Quincy's demise on the farm next door," he said quietly. "We've reason to believe he had an accomplice. You haven't seen any strangers around lately, or people who wouldn't normally be on your farm?"

"Nobody I haven't seen before." Mrs. Dash's cheeks flamed bright red.

"That's fine. It never hurts to ask." Joe pulled out his smile this time. "You won't have a problem with me and Doc here taking a wander over your lands, do you? You know I'd never be one for disturbing stock and I'll be sure to leave all the gates as I find them."

Mrs. Dash's eyes flickered to the wall clock and then the stove where a big pot of something delicious was cooking. "I don't mind at all, if you think it's necessary. If you see my Brian and the boys, let them know their lunch is ready."

"I will do." Joe held out his hand for Doc who was still seated. "Come on, babe. We'll take a quick look around, so I can report back to Rocky that I've done it, and then I'll take you back to town for lunch. What do you say?"

"That I've done more walking since you claimed me, than I've ever done in my life." Doc laughed to show he was joking as he got up from his chair. "Thank you for the coffee, Mrs. Dash. Rosie, you remind your mom to be in my office in two more days and I can take that cast off, okay?"

"Two more sleeps." Rosie jumped up and down. "Can you cut out the lovely unicorn picture for me like you did last time?"

"Your dad is very clever at making your cast look so pretty," Doc agreed. "I won't ruin it when we take it off your arm. Now, you be good for your mom and I'll see you soon. Mrs. Dash." Doc nodded.

"Thank you, Doc." Mrs. Dash seemed happier now they were talking about other things. "We'll see you soon."

/~/~/~/~/

"Okay," Doc hissed as they walked past the house barn headed for the hills beyond. "What was all that about? I thought you weren't going to mention the investigation?"

"I wasn't," Joe said calmly, latching the gate behind them and reaching out his hand. Doc took it, not because he was under any illusions this was a romantic stroll, but because he needed the connection. "Rosie is worried about her dad. She wasn't specific, and I didn't question her, if that's what you're worried about, but she wanted to know what happened to people when they did bad things. She told me we should look in the old barn at the back of the property and then reminded me her dad was one of the good guys."

"Mrs. Dash was as nervous as a cat on a hot plate," Doc said, matching Joe stride for stride across the grass. "Is there a chance Myron's got some hold on Brian, or one of his sons?"

"I don't know, but we need to talk to Brian. Preferably alone and away from where anyone might see us. I don't want anyone to hurt that wee girl and her family."

Looking around, Doc couldn't see any sign of anyone anywhere, but that didn't mean someone wasn't watching them. The problem was, his animal half was damn good at letting him know when strangers were near, but disregarded people he knew. As a doctor, he knew just about everyone in town. His heart sank at the idea Brian was their mole. Doc had only ever known him as a good man, just like his little girl believed.

They must have walked for about ten minutes when Joe stopped them at the top of a small hill. "The Forest farm is that way," he said pointing to his right. "You can just see the roof of his house from here. Robert was killed in that third paddock from the house, over there where it meets the Dash's land. The Dash's far boundary is that way," he moved his arm to the left. "The old barn Rosie told me to check out is just down that gully, tucked under the brow of that hill."

"That's not much of a distance for a running shifter," Doc said, looking between the two points. "Someone could have easily climbed the Forest fence line, coated Robert's horns and run back before anyone noticed. Knowing Forest and his mean attitude, he didn't call the department for a while, thinking he could solve the problem himself. That delay would have given the accomplice plenty of time to hide on Dash's property, especially if he was being helped by someone who lives here. I don't suppose anyone thought to check at the time?"

"Rocky and Mal backed me up when we got the call, but with me down, Robert dead and old man Forest grumbling about his damaged fence, no one would have thought to look. There was no reason at that time to think Robert was working with someone else."

"Seeing it from this perspective, definitely means the theory is plausible." Doc immediately scanned the area as he felt Joe stiffen.

"There're voices coming from the barn," Joe whispered.

"Brian and two of his sons are supposed to be there," Doc said, lowering his voice as well. "It could be them."

"If it is, then Dash is having a right beef with one of the boys. Someone's fighting. Come on." Joe took off, sprinting down the hill, leaving Doc no choice but to follow. He would rather they crept closer – listened to what was going on instead of running hell for leather into a known fight. But then, this was Joe's job, something Doc knew he was going to have to reconcile himself with sooner or later. At least Joe wouldn't be facing any of this on his own, because if one person laid a hand on his mate, Arrowtown would quickly learn what a pissed off lizard could do.

Chapter Sixteen

Joe didn't want to drag his mate into an altercation. That was the last thing he wanted. But he was hard wired to respond if he heard sounds of violence, and those sounds were getting clearer with every step he took. Someone was getting beaten. It would have to be buffalos. There's no way a man who'd take the time to draw a purple unicorn on his daughter's cast, would take his sons out to a remote barn and lay into them.

And he was right. Al had Brian caught in a headlock while Wall was punching the crap out of Roe and Carmine. The deer shifters were putting up a good fight, but like all deer shifters, they were slight of build and Wall was aptly named. "Sheriff's office," Joe yelled as he charged towards his biggest cousin. "Stand down, or I'll take you in."

"Nothing going on here." Wall and Al both stepped back and holding up their hands as Roe and Carmine ran to their father, who was rubbing his neck. "Just a friendly brawl between friends."

"You're not our friend, asshole." Roe, the youngest of the three deer shifters yelled out. "You forced us to hide you. You threatened Mom and little Rosie."

"Roe...Don't...." Brian rasped. "Joe's one of them."

"Deputy Joe's one of the finest men in this town," Doc said angrily, striding over and knocking Brian's hand away from his throat so he could examine him. "If you're going to sit there, spouting shit about my mate, your throat is about to feel a lot worse."

"Dad can't help it," Carmine whispered. "That human lawyer filled his head with lies and fake promises, spreading all this shit about how Deputy Joe killed Robert in cold blood and then saying it was Dad's duty as a loyal Arrowtown citizen to help Robert's sons get their revenge."

"You two have no right to be here," Joe said sternly, keeping his eye on his cousins. They weren't the brightest bulbs in the box, but they had a mean streak a mile wide. "Your family was banished and the whole town agreed. I'm taking you in."

"You and who's army, ass-wipe?" Wall sneered as he slapped one fist into his open palm. "We used to trash your butt all the time when we was young. What makes you think you can make us do anything now?"

"Because my mate just called for backup and you might have beaten me when I was a teenager, but I'm not that scared kid anymore."

"You've got a mate?" Al's mouth dropped open in shock. "How come you got one before we did? We're older than you. How come I haven't got one?"

"Stop thinking with your dick, dickhead," Wall scowled at his brother. "Dad's dead, remember? And this asshole killed him. He's the only thing stopping us from coming home."

"Sheriff Rocky might have a thing to say about that, as might the people who bought your family houses fair and square when you were banished," Joe snapped. "Just because you're big, don't think for one second any Quincy will be allowed back into Arrowtown – whether I'm dead or not."

"But you're a Quincy too." Al scratched his head.

"Not anymore, I'm not. I'm a Farriday, as in Doctor Nathan Farriday's mate. Now, shut up and put your hands behind your back for cuffing." Joe knew it was a long shot, but then his cousins were distracted. Sure enough, Al, probably still fretting about his lack of mate, put his hands behind his back and Joe had the cuffs on him before he could blink. That evened the odds a bit.

Wall strode over and slapped his brother around the head. "What did you do that for?" Al tried to rub his head, but of course, he couldn't.

"Now, I've got to fight him to get the damn keys, knucklehead. Didn't Uncle Myron teach you nothing?"

"But Joe's the Deputy. Dad always said follow a deputy's orders and he'd make things right at the office."

"Dad doesn't run that office anymore, shit for brains," Wall yelled. "He's dead! Joe killed him."

"Yeah, but Joe's still a deputy, right?"

"As fun as this all is, watching you two re-enact something from dumb and dumber," Joe said firmly. "Wall, I need you to put your arms behind your back for me."

Wall spun around swinging. Joe expected that and ducked quickly. He'd grown up watching Wall tackle everything with his fists. His real name was Wallace, but no one had called him by his full name since he was five and bloodied the nose of two rabbit shifters on his first day of school. Joe drove his fist, using all his strength into Wall's podgy middle and then as Wall bent over with an "oomph" Joe clasped both his hands together and smashed them into the back of Wall's head.

"You bastard," Wall screamed, dropping to his knees and rubbing his head. Unfortunately, he didn't stay down, pushing himself off the ground and charging like the buffalo he was. Side stepping just in time, Joe kicked him as he went passed, but it barely had an impact as Wall crashed into the side of the old barn. Planks smashed under his weight, and Joe thought he'd gone down. But Wall grabbed hold of a broken support beam and came back swinging the four foot length like a baseball bat.

"You always thought you were too damn good for the rest of us," Wall snarled. "Getting an education. Wearing a uniform. Butter wouldn't melt on your super smooth tongue, would it?"

"I'll try it and let you know." Joe was watching Wall's hand swinging the beam. "You aren't going to win this fight, Wall."

"I never lose." Yelling like a demented Viking, Wall raised the beam above his head and charged again. Hunching his shoulders, Joe crouched down and as Wall came forward he turned, pushing the full weight of his shoulder into Wall's belly. A resounding crack over his back made Joe grunt, but he wasn't giving up. Digging in with his boots, Joe called on the spirit of his buffalo and put everything he could into his shoulder. The beam hit him across the back of his thighs this time and Joe stumbled, but as he braced himself for another blow he heard a low guttural growl. Everything went deathly still.

"What the fuck is that?" Wall backed away, his face white, the beam he'd been wielding falling from his hand. Snatching it up, in case Wall got it into his head to attack the menacing lizard moving in on them, Joe pulled a second set of cuffs from his pocket.

"That, cousin, is my mate, and in case you didn't read the memo, his kind feast on ours. That makes you his prey. One bite and you'll be in agony for days, your body slowly rotting thanks to his venom and the wicked bacteria he has in his jaws. There'll be nothing you can do to stop it. When the venom has burrowed into your flesh, the poison will hit your bloodstream and in less than two minutes after that, you'll be dead."

Joe wasn't sure of the last part, but Wall didn't know that. "Put your arms behind your back, or I'll just walk away and leave him to it."

"But shifters don't eat each other. I'm in my human form. He's a doctor. He's supposed to save lives," Wall wailed, backing up as the Komodo advanced.

"Which is the only reason you're not dead now." Joe jingled the cuffs in his hand. "Arms behind your back, or I'll walk away."

"Don't let him eat me." Wall shrieked as Doc growled again. "I'll do it. I'll do it. Put me in protective custody. I'll tell you everything I know about the raid, the bombing, everything, just don't let him come near me."

"What about our dear Uncle Myron?" Joe snapped the cuffs on hard, knowing they'd hurt, but damn, his back and thighs were still throbbing and would likely be bruised by dinner time.

"Anything. Just...."

"Fucking hell, would you look at that?" A new voice joined the scene. Joe looked up to see Rocky and Mal had joined them, Rocky sporting a big hunting rifle over his shoulder. "Doc, you've got hidden talents."

Doc growled, only this time it was aimed at Rocky. Shit. Pushing Wall to the ground, Joe dived in front of his mate, holding out his arms. "Don't say anything, don't antagonize him. Yes, he's cognizant, but Doc's hidden his secret for centuries and he only shifted because Wall was attacking me. How many people would go to him for medical treatment if they knew he could kill them?"

"I would," Brian piped up from where he was still sitting with his sons. Joe had forgotten the deer shifters were even there. "Anyone who can make a full grown buffalo shifter shit his pants, is worth having as a friend. Doc's been treating my kids since Carmine here was born. That ain't gonna change."

"I appreciate that, Brian," Joe said, nodding in their direction. "But surely you can see, if news got out, some people are going to be scared of him."

"We're not going to say anything," Mal said, laughing as the Komodo's head bunted Joe's hand, looking for a scratch. "I'm sure Brian and his family can keep the secret too. Although, Mr. Dash, I have to say, things are not looking good for you right now. Harboring two known fugitives can carry a nasty penalty."

"My cousins threatened their Mom and little Rosie, if they didn't do as they were told," Joe said quickly, flicking his hand at Wall and Al. "It was Rosie who warned me I should come out here. She told me there were bad men here, but she also reminded me her dad is one of the good guys."

"I've been so anxious about all this," Brian said, his eyes damp. "Yelling at the missus and the wee one too. I didn't know what to do. It's not as though we could stop them, and I didn't dare leave the farm to warn anyone in case my ladies got hurt. These two, they've done nothing wrong." Brian indicated his two sons who were watching Doc, absolutely fascinated. "All we did was let them stay at the barn and bring them food."

"Then who the hell has been watching us in town and feeding these two information?" Rocky snapped. "Because, sure as hell, someone is."

"That was me." Carmine twisted his hands, his face a mask of misery. "I'm sorry, Dad, but Al said he'd do nasty sexual stuff to me if I didn't. I didn't know they were going to blow up the sheriff's office or that Deputy Joe would get shot."

"Hey," Wall yelled out. "We were here when that office was bombed."

"It's okay, son," Brian said awkwardly, tucking his son under his arm as he faced Rocky proudly. "We'll take whatever punishments owing to us. I know we did wrong."

"And sometimes good people do bad things because bad people make them do it, isn't that right, Deputy Joe?" Rocky grinned. "Yep, we stopped by the house before we came over here. I talked to Rosie too. I'm half inclined to give her a badge. Mr. Dash, boys. I will need to talk to you all. Tomorrow will be fine. I just want your corroborating testimony for our records. I don't see any reason for anyone in your family to be charged over this. However, I do have one suggestion."

"What is it? Anything." Brian looked as though he was ready to cry again.

"Get that young Rosie a cell phone and program the Sheriff's number into it." Rocky grinned, showing all his teeth. "That little one has got eyes like a hawk and ears like a wolf. She'll make a good deputy one day."

"Thank you, Sheriff. Thank you, thank you."

Ignoring Brian and his cuffed cousins, Joe looked down at his mate. "Did you shred your clothes, babe, or are they still in one piece? I'm not sure you're going to fit in the car like that."

"You mean these?" Mal laughed as he held up the ripped remains of Doc's clothes. "Here," he said, throwing Joe a set of keys. "Take the SUV. If you put the back seats down, he should fit, or maybe not. But there's a spare blanket in the back which should keep him covered until you get back to the surgery."

"Let's hope Rosie's down for an afternoon nap," Joe whispered as he and his scaled companion started back across the paddocks. "Otherwise we won't be home until sundown. I think it's about damn time you claimed my ass, don't you?"

It was really amazing just how fast a Komodo dragon could run when he had the incentive. Joe laughed as he chased after him. This wasn't quite

the run he'd envisaged with his mate,
but it was close.

Chapter Seventeen

Doc rubbed his belly as he closed his surgery door. Having missed his morning appointments, his afternoon wasn't spent loving on his mate in their big comfortable bed, but rather sewing back on a toe, reassuring two rabbits who came in to confirm their pregnancies and performing emergency surgery on a young wolf shifter who hadn't bothered to remove the plastic wrapper from a chocolate bar he'd stolen from his mother's stash.

Glancing upstairs, he smiled as he heard pots and pans being clattered about. Joe had spent a good part of the afternoon at the mayor's office, which was now the temporary home for the sheriff's department too and then came back with an armful of groceries. He wanted to cook Doc dinner. Just thinking about it gave Doc a warm glow inside.

Heading back into his surgery, Doc cleaned up, making sure all waste was properly disposed of and his instruments were secure in the sterilization tank. He'd been that busy, he hadn't had a chance to fully process the events from earlier in the day, but now, as he did, he slumped onto his rolling stool, burying his face in his hands.

I shifted in front of other people. Decades. It'd been decades, possibly longer since Doc shifted in front of another person – except for Joe of course. Joe would keep his secrets safe. In fact, Doc's cheeks flushed as he remembered Joe standing in front of him as if protecting his lizard from judgmental eyes. *It is what it is,* he realized, thinking about it now. If they had to move to another town, or people stopped coming to him because they were scared of his shifted form, then he'd deal with that issue when it happened.

Doc hadn't had a choice and that helped put the whole morning into perspective. When he saw Wall swing at Joe with a hunk of wood, there was no thinking involved. Secrecy was the last thing on his mind. No one was going to swing a weapon at his mate and get away with it. He'd never shifted so fast in his life and he'd remember the look of fear on Wall's face for a long time to come – it was a memory guaranteed to put a smile on his face.

Doc thought about the other thing quietly plaguing his mind since that morning. He looked over at the cupboard where he stored his supplies. *It can wait until tomorrow,* he thought, getting out of his chair. Joe had dinner ready, and barring any emergencies, Doc would finally get the chance to claim his mate properly. *Someone had better be dying if they want to interrupt me tonight.* He adjusted his filling cock as he slowly climbed the stairs.

/~/~/~/~/

Joe pottered around the kitchen, wincing as he moved too far one way.

There wasn't a lot left he had to do. The roast was resting on the top of the stove, the vegetables crisp and ready to serve in the oven. He'd heard the front door close and lock downstairs and knew his mate would be coming up soon. *He's going to need a hearty meal,* Joe thought with a smile, the plug he had in his butt keeping him in a state of constant arousal.

It wasn't as though he meant to go snooping through his mate's things. After a long and frustrating afternoon listening to his cousins blame everyone from Myron to the Fates for their actions, which included organizing Hargraves's escape and the bombing of the Sheriff's office, no one was any closer to finding out where Myron was hiding or what his Uncle's motivation was.

Thoroughly sick of listening to them bitch and moan about how nothing was actually their fault – Rocky fed them, then ordered them to be chained in the basement of the Mayor's building, naked, bound in Simon's special cuffs so they couldn't shift or get out of them by any means, and basically left them to stew for the night. Glad to escape, Joe grabbed just enough goodies to make a roast meal, all under the beady eyes of Mrs. Hooper, and headed back to Doc's for a shower.

But he didn't have any clean clothes with him, and that led to him looking for something of his mates to wear – which meant going through his dresser and finding…toys. Lots of toys. Joe's eyes had bugged out when he found an entire drawer full of things that usually graced the shelves of an adult shop. Floggers, plugs and dildos of all sizes, some weird clamp things Joe had never seen before and leather cuffs – some with chains and some without.

Yeah, Joe had slammed the drawer shut as fast as he'd opened it, his cheeks flaming. Pulling out a pair of sweats from another drawer, Joe's fingers had lingered on the toy drawer. Those plugs looked really tempting and one of them was still in its packaging, so it hadn't been used. *You'd be doing your mate a favor, prepping yourself.* It wasn't that Joe didn't trust Doc to do a thorough job himself, but...wearing a plug to prepare for his mate was daring...totally out of his comfort zone, and that's why Joe had to do it. Doc had done it for him and didn't even blush.

What he hadn't counted on was how the damn plug sent shivers through his prostate every time he moved. Getting the plug inside himself was a novel experience, but wearing it, while doing something simple like preparing a meal – there was no way Joe could ignore the sensations. Even chopping vegetables became an erotic experience. Every time Joe walked, his prostate sang and when he bent over to check the roast meat in the oven he was conscious of an unfamiliar heavy fullness and the strong urge to clench his ass muscles. A tickle ran from his balls to his hole and at the time, Joe had squeaked before looking around hurriedly to make sure Doc wasn't around.

Come on. Come on. Joe looked up at the wall clock. It'd been ten minutes since he'd heard the door locking. *I do hope my mate's not fretting about this morning.* Because that would be the sort of thing Joe could see Doc doing. He was just debating if he should go downstairs and see for himself when he heard Doc's tread on the stairs. That's when self-doubt decided to slap him around the head.

Oh my god, Doc's going to think I'm some kind of a slut. I'll hurt his feelings because he'll think I didn't trust him to look after me. Oh my god, I need to get to the bathroom and take it out…but then he'll still know. He's a doctor. What if my hole is still loose? He'll think I've been lying to him about being a virgin. Shit. Shit. Shit. Why did I do this?

"Hey, babe. Are you okay?" Doc was there, right in front of him and Joe felt like a blithering idiot. He opened his mouth, but words wouldn't come out. And then Doc's scent hit him, and he realized his mate was as horny as he was, and there went his ass, clenching all over again.

"I need to kiss you!" Flinging his arms around Doc's neck, Joe felt his need rising. His skin was tight, his cock hardened to the point of pain. The butt plug was part of the reason, but in reality, it was all Doc's presence – it'd always been Doc.

/~/~/~/~/

Doc felt the fire in his balls spread as he brushed against his mate's warm lips. The scent of Joe's arousal battled on his tongue along with the roast meat and cooking vegetables. But even if he hadn't eaten for a week, nothing was more potent than the smell of aroused mate. Doc didn't have a clue what had his mate tied up in knots when he walked in, but now was not the time for conversation.

Or food apparently. Caught up in Doc's kiss, Joe still had the wherewithal to turn off the oven. "Take me here," Joe whispered as he pulled back, his voice ragged with lust, his lips spit-slicked and swollen. "I've been ready for two freaking hours. I'm going to burst."

Not exactly the claiming scene I'd envisaged. Doc was old, but he was no fool. Sliding his hands down Joe's back, he pushed his fingers under the waistband of sweats he recognized as his. Joe's butt muscles were as tight as a rock. Doc wanted to slap them to see if they'd jiggle but instead he curled his fingers around, pushing them into Joe's tight crack. He quickly found the source of Joe's discomfort.

"Oh, babe, I don't deserve you." Doc bit back a moan as his cock leaked.

"You're not mad at me for finding your stash?" Joe looked up from where he was busy unbuttoning Doc's shirt.

"Fucking grateful." Shoving Joe's sweats down his thighs, Doc shuffled him backwards and lifted him onto the kitchen counter before pulling the sweats off all the way. "Lie back," he growled, as he dropped the sweats on the floor. "I have to see."

Pushing the plates, he'd left out to dish up on aside, Joe rested his elbows on the counter, his face the color of beetroot. "Hmm," Doc traced around the black silicon that contrasted so beautifully with Joe's skin. "You went with the biggest one I had. I would've loved to see you get that in that tight hole."

"It wasn't easy, but then you're not exactly small." Joe bit his lip.

"Hey." Doc leaned forward and pecked Joe on the lips before ripping off his shirt. He heard a button ping, but as long as it didn't go near the food he didn't care. "You, my mate, are fucking incredible." He shoved his pants down to his ankles and fisted his cock. "Just thinking about you does this to me."

Griping Joe's bent thighs, Doc pulled him, so his butt rested on the edge of the counter. *The perfect height.* Catching the edge of the plug, he pulled it out a short way and then pushed it back in, wiggling it as he did so.

Joe's groan came from his balls. "Don't tease, please," he begged. "Do you have any idea what it's like trying to cook with this thing in me?"

Doc could imagine, having done it himself a time or two, but he wasn't mean enough to tease. Not when Joe's balls were already tight, and his cock was thumping a wee tattoo on Joe's abs in time with his harsh panting. Taking care to go slow, Doc grabbed the edges of the plug and pulled. The one Joe'd chosen flared in the middle and seeing how the plug stretched Joe's hole wide as it came out had Doc sending a vote of thanks to the Fates. Joe truly was perfect for him in every way.

"Empty," Joe moaned as the plug fell free.

"Not for long." Swiping enough of the residual lube from the plug, Doc coated the head of his dick and thrust forward. The squeeze around his cock was indescribable and rather than push any further, Doc widened Joe's hips as far as they would go, leaning forward so he could taste his mate's lips.

"You," he said nibbling softly, "mean the world to me."

"Does that mean you love me?" Joe's dark eyes were intense.

"It's impossible not to." Doc was never one for fancy words, but in that moment, he would've given Joe his soul without question. "Breathe out slowly." Despite the plug, Joe's ass was still tight, and Doc rocked his way slowly inside, determined his brave mate wouldn't suffer a moment's discomfort.

"We need to buy a bigger plug," Joe gasped when Doc was half way in. "Already full."

"You were made for me. You can take it," Doc grunted as he pushed the last inches inside and froze. He didn't dare look down. If he caught one glimpse of the way Joe stretched around him, he'd blow. Instead he studied his mate's handsome face. Flushed, red cheeked, his eyes bright and his lips darker than usual, Doc knew the word love could in no way describe the depth of what he was feeling. "Everything," he whispered. "You are everything to me."

Reaching out, Doc caught Joe around the neck and pulled his torso closer. His lizard stirred, poised, waiting, Joe's neck calling to him. Doc had a momentary flash of fear – what if...? But then Joe groaned and wiggled his hips and Doc had to move. Determined to treat his mate as more than a hole to fuck, Doc's thrusts were sharp, stabbing motions that sped up as Joe's hole relaxed. But he refused to let go of Joe's nape. He wanted Joe to know he was loving on his whole body. They bumped noses, sharing breath, both panting loud enough to rival a train.

"Oh, gods, right there," Joe panted as Doc hit his stride. "Right there!"

One hand on Joe's hip to steady him, the other clasped firmly around Joe's neck, Doc dared to look down and groaned at the sight. It was obscene the way Joe's body flexed and held him tight, and yet it was more beautiful than anything in Doc's long life. Part of it was their mating bond, sure, but Doc knew it was more than that. He couldn't feel this way with any other. Only Joe. Only Joe. "Oh, my gods, Joe." Doc's cry was ragged, but his orgasm blindsided him. His teeth were in Joe's neck before he knew what was happening, his animal roaring in his head as he was finally allowed the claiming he'd been waiting for.

Blood. Joe's blood coated his tongue and that was enough to snap Doc from his orgasm-stupor. Joe's body was trembling, and he cried out. The smell of spunk hit the air as Doc removed his teeth with as much haste as he dared. *Please, please, please,* he prayed with everything he was, licking over the jagged wound. He'd never known of another Komodo dragon to take a true mate. He'd never bitten his late wife. Joe flopping his head back with a long groan didn't help.

"Joe. Joe!" He said frantically, cradling Joe's head and bringing it upright. "Are you all right? Talk to me, god damnit, talk to me."

"You expect me to talk after the best sex of my life?" Joe's smile was goofy, and his eyes were wide, his pupils blown. "Damn. If people knew what your bite could do, they'd be queuing up."

"You're not hurt?" Doc scanned the bite. It was already healing, as a mating bite would, leaving behind a wicked scar. "You don't feel any pain, nausea or headaches?"

"I see rainbows," Joe giggled. Holding up his finger he went to tap Doc's nose and missed. "Lot's of sparkling lights and rainbows."

Burying his face in Joe's shoulder, Doc's shoulders shook with relief. It seemed when a Komodo dragon took a true mate, their bite acted like a hallucinogenic drug. With luck, the effects were only temporary, but inside Doc was overwhelmed. His darkest fear had been pulled into the light. All his life he'd feared taking a true mate – scared beyond belief that his bite would prove lethal to the person he loved. Holding Joe tight, he felt strong arms wrap around him clumsily, even while his mate was still giggling. A hug. It was exactly what he needed. The cleanup, dinner and everything else in their life could just wait five minutes.

Chapter Eighteen

"Hey, babe, did I miss dinner?" Joe woke slowly, shaking the muzzy feeling from his head. "Man, that was buzzy." He looked around. He was in bed, but Doc was nowhere to be seen. A quick glance at the window showed it was still dark out. Joe had no idea how late or early it was. "Doc. Nathan," he called out softly, straining his ears for a reply. Pushing himself upright, Joe had to stop for a moment – he'd never had a hangover, but he imagined he had all the symptoms. Reaching up, he traced the ridged scar on the side of his neck. The shiver that ran through his body was unexpectedly sexy. But then his stomach grumbled loudly, reminding him he hadn't had any of the lovely roast meal he'd cooked for his mate.

"Where is he?" Joe muttered as he forced his legs to work. "You'd think when a guy takes another guy's virginity he'd at least stick around for a cuddle afterwards." But even as he said it Joe knew he was being unfair. He had no idea how long he'd been sleeping. Doc had cared for him. He'd been put to bed, no doubt because he was too loopy to get there himself, and apart from the new scar and the ache in his butt when he stood up, there was no other evidence of their claiming, which meant Doc, "Nathan," Joe reminded himself, had cleaned him up before letting him sleep.

Standing was an interesting concept. For a moment, Joe thought he'd fall, but as he stretched out his arms and back, he could feel his strength returning and the fuzziness of his brain seeped away. Making his way slowly to the bathroom, Joe took care of his most pressing need and then wandered out through the bedroom and looked around the apartment. There was no sign of his missing mate, but there was a covered plate on the kitchen counter. Joe eyed it, weighing up his options – it was tempting, but he knew the food would never sit right in his stomach until he knew where his mate had disappeared to.

Checking the spare room – very impersonal and empty of living beings, Joe rested his hand on the stairway wall as he made his way downstairs. It crossed his mind his mate could be working, in which case he might not want to be disturbed. But Joe shook that nonsense out of his head. He wasn't going to let his insecurities impact his relationship. Nathan cared for him, and if he was busy then Joe would steal a quick kiss and go back upstairs and enjoy the meal left for him.

The waiting room was dark, but Joe could see easily enough. There was a strip of light showing under the treatment door though. Again, Joe hesitated. What if Doc was busy working on an emergency? But if that was the case, the waiting room light would be on and there would be people around. Joe didn't pick up any fresh scents and a quick glance confirmed the front door was still locked.

Knocking quietly, Joe opened the treatment room door and poked his head around it. The last thing he expected to see was Doc hunched over his computer at his desk, tears streaming down his face. "Babe. Oh, shit babe, what's wrong?" Joe hurried to Doc's side, pulling him off the chair and into his arms.

"I'm so sorry." Doc hiccupped and tried again. "There's no information. I can't find a damn thing. I've been searching for hours and there's nothing."

"Babe, what are you talking about?" Joe never dreamed it was possible for his mate to be this upset. Doc was usually unflappable. "Is this about me going all loopy on you when you bit me? You didn't hurt me. I swear, nothing hurts. There's no permanent damage. I'm fine."

"There was that." Doc rested his cheek on Joe's shoulder and his hands landed lightly on Joe's hip bones. "I was worried. I'd never heard of anyone having that type of reaction to a Komodo bite before. So, I thought I'd do some research, you know." He hiccupped again and swiped a hand over his damp cheeks. "I needed to be certain there were no long-lasting effects. But then I took the test and it was staring me in the face and I searched and searched, and I can't find anything about my kind anywhere. There's nothing. It's like I don't exist."

"Hush, babe, it'll be all right. You can see for yourself I'm fine." Joe stroked Doc's hair. "I felt a bit fuzzy when I woke up, but it cleared as soon as I started moving around. I loved the experience, seriously, but if you're that worried then you just don't have to bite me anymore. I'm claimed now – you claimed me and that's the most important thing." He held his mate close for a moment and then the rest of what Doc said hit him. "Hang on a minute, did you say test? What test was that? Are you okay? Did this test hurt you in some way? Was the biting bad for you?"

"No, nothing like that. I was acting on another hunch I had. It's that test over there." Doc tilted his head in the direction of the bench where he kept his equipment. It was bare except for one white stick. Joe's heart jumped. Encouraging Doc to move with him, Joe went over and picked it up. There was a small panel showing two blue lines in the shape of a cross.

"Babe, is this what I think it is?" Joe kept his voice calm, refusing to jump to conclusions. "This isn't a test for cancer or some other deadly disease is it?"

"No. I'm like you. I don't get human diseases." Doc looked straight at him, his voice devoid of emotion. "That test means I'm pregnant. I can't tell you how many we're having, I can't even tell you when. I don't know if

I'm going to have eggs or live babies. I just know the test is positive. We're going to be parents."

"Honestly? You can tell that so soon?" Joe's happy shout was loud in the quiet room. "We're going to have a baby. That's wonderful news." Picking Doc up, Joe swung him around the room laughing as loudly as he did when he'd been bitten. Maybe there was a residual effect from Doc's bite after all, but Joe didn't care. They were going to be parents and he was over-the-moon happy about it.

/~/~/~/~/

It was really hard not to get swept up in Joe's enthusiasm, and Doc hated being a grouch about the whole thing. But just the thought of being pregnant made his stomach threaten to revolt and his head felt like it was splitting open. It wasn't that he didn't like kids, as such. He'd had three of his own and had brought hundreds of babies into the world. He just never thought he'd be the one carrying them. Although when he saw the positive test result he could have slapped himself. All non-furry shifters could get pregnant, regardless of gender. As a doctor that was one of the first things he'd learned. But Doc hadn't been kidding when he said he couldn't find any information about the breeding habits of his kind and that could pose a problem.

"Babe." Doc hated to wipe the beaming smile from his mate's lovely face, but they had to talk. "Have you eaten dinner yet? There's some things we should probably discuss."

Joe seemed to catch on quick that Doc wasn't quite as happy about their news as he was. "Of course. Come on, we'll go upstairs. I wanted to find you when I woke up, so I haven't eaten yet, but more importantly, have you had anything?"

"You cooked a wonderful roast and I enjoyed every mouthful, thank you." Doc smiled.

"Is this...can you...I know we need to talk." Joe stopped them both at the foot of the stairs, his face grave. "But can you tell me now? Are you happy about becoming a parent again?"

The sixty four thousand dollar question. Joe will smell a lie. "I'm not averse to it, especially with you," Doc said, choosing his words carefully. "When I first suspected, the morning after you claimed me, I could imagine the pair of us raising children together. I just, this has thrown me for a bit of a loop. I don't know anything about how our kind deliver and raise their young."

"So, you're not strictly unhappy as such." Trust Joe to want confirmation. "You're just unsure on what's going to happen. And I'm guessing this has to do with your own upbringing. You're right. We should head upstairs. My stomach is ready to eat through my spinal cord, and you need to sit down. Have you had any sleep? I don't even know what time it is."

"Just after three in the morning." Doc turned off the surgery light and followed his mate upstairs. "That seems to be a type of witching hour for us. The time for deep conversations."

"At least we won't get disturbed." Joe's flash of teeth helped settle the turmoil in Doc's heart. He waited until they were both seated at the kitchen counter – he with a cup of coffee in his hand, and damn, he was going to have to restrict his intake on that too now he was pregnant, and Joe hoeing into his reheated meal.

Staring out of the window at the quiet streets below, Doc said softly, "I don't know where I came from. Now I'm pregnant, that lack of knowledge scares me."

"You never met your parents at all?"

Doc shook his head. "I used to think I was the only one, but Darwin, you know, Simon's mate, told me once the same thing happened to Simon.

He was born in snake form and didn't realize he was a shifter until he changed during puberty. It was a hell of a shock to him. One I could relate to, although I never said anything at the time."

"I remember, when I was learning about natural Komodo dragons, that they usually hatch out of eggs and then spend the first four years of their lives up a tree, so they don't get eaten by others like them."

"Now you can see my concern," Doc said drily. "However, there's another problem, from what little I can remember of my childhood. You have to remember, I was in my animal form. I didn't know anything about the human world at that time. But when I did shift – I estimate I was about fifteen at the time – I had to get out of the area in a hurry. None of my so-called brothers and sisters shifted like I did, and I became instant prey."

"That's unusual." Joe popped the last piece of potato in his mouth and pushed his plate aside, reaching for Doc's hand. Swallowing, he said, "maybe you were just the first one of your clutch to mature enough to shift."

"I thought the same thing," Doc agreed. "After I'd shifted, I hung around, living in trees, watching some of my siblings. By this stage we were fully adult and preferred being on our own. I don't remember ever mating with a female, but we'd meet up over a carcass once in a while. I never saw anyone on two legs until long after I'd left the area."

"I can't imagine what that must have been like." Joe's hand was warm on his and Doc gripped it gently.

"I spent years hiding," Doc said, thinking back. "I came across a village, this was on Komodo Island, centuries ago. There were barely any people living there, but I found some. Unfortunately, I quickly learned my

302

differences meant I wasn't welcome among their kind."

"Your torso?" Joe's eyes were full of sympathy.

"And the silver in my hair. I was probably thirty, maybe thirty five, before I learned to keep my body covered. There wasn't much I could do about my hair, but I took to moving around – finally found a small pack of wolf shifters I stayed with and they taught me how to hide in plain sight. I started learning about medicine from their shaman and found I had a knack for it, and things blossomed from there."

There were a lot of other things Doc learned in that pack too, but his mate didn't need to hear about any of that. Suffice to say, once he'd met his late wife, he was living in America as a fully qualified doctor – as much as one could be qualified in those days – and fully conversant on the medical needs of a wide range of shifters.

"Is this why you're worried about having our child?" Joe asked, almost hesitantly. "Because you're worried about laying eggs?"

"I don't know what's going to happen, or even what to expect." Doc could feel the events of the day and night catching up with him. "That's why I was researching council records. There are no known instances of a Komodo dragon shifter in any publicly available information online and nothing in the medical database." He raised his hand to cover a yawn.

"I think it's time you were in bed," Joe said firmly. "From what I remember from my reading about natural dragons, eggs can take up to nine months to hatch from when they're laid which is about the same length of pregnancy for a human. Buffalo calves can take just as long to be born. We've got plenty of time to work things out."

"What if I start laying eggs while I'm sleeping?" Doc didn't really think that was possible – he didn't have the right equipment for a start, but he was curious to see what Joe's response would be.

"I'll put a towel down on the sheets," Joe said with a smirk. "But if it turns out you're pooping instead of laying eggs, you can clean it up yourself."

"You're all heart," Doc chuckled. *At least I won't be going through this alone,* he thought as he let Joe lead him to their bedroom. And yes, that was a comforting thought.

Chapter Nineteen

It was after lunch when Joe made his way to the Sheriff department's temporary offices. Determined to ensure Doc slept in for a change, Joe turned off his mate's alarm clock and sat down in the waiting room during Doc's morning surgery hours, encouraging the few people who popped in to come back during the afternoon session. Gossip had traveled fast, as it did in Arrowtown, and most people were aware Doc had been with him during an altercation on Dash's farm. No one asked Joe about his mate's shifter status though, and Joe was hopeful Brian and his family would continue to keep the secret.

The first person he saw in the office was Liam, dressed in his uniform, his feet up on the desk Mal had been using. "Hi there, stranger," Liam grinned. "How's mated life treating you?"

"Much the same as it does you, I imagine," Joe said with an easy smile. Since Liam, Trent and Beau had their first child, the lion shifter was a lot more relaxed about life. "Where are Rocky and Mal?"

"Down in the basement, working out some aggression if I know Rocky." Liam slapped his fist into his open palm. "It seems Dumb and Dumber didn't get any wiser overnight. They keep telling us they don't know where this mysterious Myron is, and apparently they haven't got a clue what Myron's plan is, but the stink of their lies is enough to make me sneeze."

"I'd be inclined to let the council guards have a go," Joe said, dropping into the nearest chair. "But we all know they don't give a shit about what happens around here."

"That might have changed now. Oh, you haven't heard." Liam's feet landed on the floor with a thump as he rested his elbows on the desk.

"Hargraves and the council liaison officer were attacked last night on their way to the Jackson airport. Word came through to the office this morning."

The hair on the back of Joe's neck stood up. "Don't tell me, both of them are dead."

"Shot straight through the head multiple times," Liam agreed, "but only the council guy. There's no sign of Hargraves anywhere and apparently the council had their best trackers out all night trying to find a trace of him. It happened about ten miles this side of Jackson."

"Oh joy." Joe scowled. "That means they'll be in here soon enough, wanting to go through all the records we haven't got thanks to our bombed offices."

"You missed them. They've been and gone," Liam laughed. "Why do you think Rocky needs some stress relief? If it wasn't for Mal, you and I would be on body hiding duties this afternoon."

Joe could well imagine it. The shifter council had been appointed fifty years before, ostensibly to work with human government and law officials and advocate for shifter rights. Arrowtown was one of the many shifter towns set up as a council initiative when it seemed some humans didn't take kindly to being reminded they weren't as strong or as fast as their shifter neighbors.

Although, there were no laws against shifters living in human towns, a lot of shifters preferred to live in a place where they weren't frowned on for walking around in their animal form. Within shifter town territories, human laws didn't apply, and each town had their own way of governing themselves. In Arrowtown, the mayor and the sheriff were elected positions, with voting held every four years. Rocky and Ra were newly elected into their positions, after some of the criminal and negligent activities by Joe's family had come to light.

When someone committed a crime, and that was rare, the town held an open meeting for all the townsfolk who suggested and voted on suitable punishments. It was during a town meeting to determine the punishment for the rabbit herd leader, Alpha Simpson and his son Gareth, after beating Ra's mate Seth nearly to death, that Ra threw his hat in the ring for contention for the Mayor's position. Joe was never sure why Rocky wanted to run for sheriff, but he was pleasantly surprised at how well the wolf had done since being elected.

"So, what happens now?" Joe forced his mind back to the present. "While Myron is still running free, no one in this town is safe and I've got a new mate to protect."

"Tell me about it. You imagine what it was like convincing my overly protective pair that I still needed to report to work after the office got bombed. I wouldn't be surprised if Trent comes running over here the moment he hears a car backfire. I want Myron stopped as much as you do."

"The problem with Myron is he's old school," Joe mused, leaning his elbows on the desk in front of him. "He stays off the grid as much as possible. Uses disposable phones left, right, and center. He pays for everything in cash and favors. I don't think he even has a bank account."

"Which makes him a lot harder to track," Liam agreed. "Would Harold know where he is?"

Joe shook his head. "I doubt it. Robert probably knew, but in the Quincy family no one told Harold anything unless they wanted it broadcast to his many mistresses." He sat up as something finally clicked in his brain. "Harold's mistresses – that's it. Whatever happened to that woman who was in Harold's office planning to help him celebrate his win? You remember, the one who thought she could seduce Rocky too?"

"I thought she lived in Jackson. Didn't Darwin know her from his stripping days?"

"Yes, that's right. Jenny, she was a cat shifter and she mentioned another woman Connie who used to service Robert when he was still in town. What about Maggie. Maybe she would know. She's still working for Ra, isn't she?"

"Ra couldn't run the office without her," Liam laughed. "He doubled her salary and begged her not to retire, which is what she'd planned to do. Damn it, we should have thought about talking to her before this."

"Then let's go and see if she can spare us a few minutes." Joe stood and smoothed the creases out of his pants. "It's not likely she's ever heard of Myron, but if his tastes for women run the same as Harold and Robert's did, then maybe we'll be in luck and get a lead."

/~/~/~/~/

Doc barely managed to hide his smile as he saw a nervous Dan sitting with a pretty rabbit shifter in his waiting room. "Come on in, the pair of you. Dan, I don't think I've met your companion."

"She's my mate, Doc." Dan stood, holding out his hand to the woman who had to be Jenny. She was pretty, with bright blond hair and intelligent eyes. "I'd like you to meet Jenny Simpson. She's the niece of the banished Alpha Simpson. Her family live in a shifter town on the coast. She came to visit after the alpha was banished and decided to stay."

"I saw you the first day I arrived in town. You don't think I was going to run out on you, even if you weren't sure who I was to you." Jenny's laugh was sweet and kind. "I understand it was you, Doc, who convinced my shy mate to ask me out on a date and to be honest with me. I can't thank you enough." She held out her hand and Doc shook it quickly before leading them into the office.

Indicating the chairs by his desk, Doc chose to sit on his rolling stool. "I'm really glad my advice helped," he said, letting his smile show this time. "Having recently claimed my mate myself, I understand how difficult it can be for a couple to be apart, especially when you both would have felt the pull to be together."

"It wasn't Dan's fault." Jenny's look at her mate was full of love. "He came and told me what was wrong with him the minute he left your office. I've never felt so proud for another person in my life. It took a lot of courage to admit something like that."

"Needless to say, Jenny's sweet rabbit confirmed what I'd hoped for." Dan's cheeks went bright red. "We found there was no need to go out for a fancy date after all. Jenny makes the best lasagna."

"You both have my heartiest congratulations. So, what are we doing here for you today? Did you want to discuss the surgical option we talked about, Dan?"

"I wasn't sure it was a good idea when Dan told me about it," Jenny admitted shyly. "I hate the idea of my mate experiencing any kind of pain and now we're mated, I'm not sure it's necessary."

"That's why we thought we'd come to you, Doc," Dan agreed. "I admit, I'd love to be able to scent my sweet mate, and any future pups we might have, but I've been without my sense of smell most of my life. I'm just worried, since the sheriff's office got blown up that maybe there's threats in this town I don't know about. What if I can't protect my mate without full use of all my senses?"

Doc shouldn't have been surprised. More than one of his clients had made veiled references to the bombing, perhaps hoping that because Doc was mated to Deputy Joe, he might know more than what was being said publicly.

Ra had put out a notice the morning after the attack, saying it was the work of humans who'd since left the area and that the sheriff's office was following every lead. He asked them all to be vigilant and to report any sightings of strangers within the territory boundaries. In the meantime, he asked for volunteers to help clear the rubble and to put anything that could be salvaged in a large container offered by the Hooper family. Even kids were out there after school, helping clear the mess brick by brick. The town was rallying together which was a positive thing to see.

"I do think this should be your decision," Doc said returning his focus to the couple in front of him. "Surgery is always a big step. The risks, seeing as you are a shifter, are minimal, but as I explained at the time, the chances of full success are also fifty fifty. While your sense of smell is important, as a wolf, your other senses will have improved over the years to counter the loss – wouldn't you agree?"

"I have better eyesight than most and can hear a pin drop a hundred yards away," Dan nodded.

"These growths Dan has in his nose," Jenny blushed prettily, "will they get worse over time? Could that endanger him in other ways?"

"How old are you, Dan?" With shifters it was always hard to tell. While Dan wasn't young, Doc could sense that, he could be aged anywhere from fifty to four hundred and fifty.

"A hundred and twenty seven," Dan mumbled as Jenny laughed.

"He thinks he's a cradle snatcher," she said patting Dan's arm. "I'm only twenty three."

"I'm sure you'll both live a long and happy life together," Doc said. "The age gap between myself and the young deputy is considerably bigger, and age is one thing very few shifters worry about. And actually Dan, I think that's a good thing – your age, I mean. The growths you have aren't very big and it's not likely they will get any bigger. It is possible they developed when you were a child, before you shifted for the first time."

Dan and Jenny shared a long look and Doc idly wondered if they had a mind link. He'd yet to try contacting Joe that way but it would be helpful if it was something they shared. He made a mental note to try later that night. He didn't know what Joe was doing as he was at work, and he didn't want to startle his mate if he was busy doing his job.

"We've decided to leave the surgery for now, Doc, if that's all right with you," Dan said finally after a long moment. "My Jenny," the pride on his face as he said those words spoke volumes, "she doesn't want to see me hurt, even intentionally, and people might talk after the surgery if I've got plaster or marks on my face."

"I might only be a rabbit, and I know my mate's a big strong wolf, but it's my job to look out for his interests, just as he does mine." Jenny smoothed her hands over her pale blue skirt before smiling up at her beaming mate. "We look after each other."

"I think you two are going to get along just fine," Doc said. "Was there anything else?" He knew there was, he could scent it. But it was up to Jenny if she wanted to say anything just yet.

"I'd like a pregnancy test please." Jenny's smile was beautiful as Dan's mouth dropped open. "My rabbit tells me we're expecting, but because my dear mate can't scent us, I want him to have something tangible he can keep, to remind him of this moment."

"You...you...you're pregnant, already?"

Doc chuckled quietly. He wished he had a camera to capture the look on Dan's face. The quiet wolf let out a whoop that could be heard at Hooper's store, standing up and swinging Jenny into his arms, much like Joe had done to him the night before. But with Dan and Jenny there were no reservations. It was a truly beautiful scene and one that reminded Doc why he got into medicine in the first place. Letting them have their moment, he found something else to do on his desk.

Chapter Twenty

Joe was alone in the temporary sheriff's office when the call came in. The chat with Maggie had been helpful to a point. Apparently, a group of young ladies used a house just outside of town limits on the main road to Jackson. A house Harold used to finance with city funds. There was a good chance the house could be empty, especially if it'd been months since someone paid the bills. But a quick chat with Darwin who was working over at Cam's suggested the girls were more likely to have found another sugar daddy than leave a perfectly good house. Liam had gone with Rocky and Mal to scope it out. It sounded like a perfect hideout for Myron and as Rocky was on the verge of killing Al and Wall, Mal thought an outing would do him good. In the meantime, Joe was going over house records for all the residents in the area, trying to think of other people Al and Wall used to knock about with when they were younger. He could have gone with them, but Doc would be expecting him home for dinner and he didn't want to be late.

"Sheriff's office, Deputy Joe speaking," he said as he put the phone to his ear.

"Deputy Joe, thank goodness you're there." Joe recognized the voice. It was Andy, his closest neighbor. "I went over to your house today to see if you had a chainsaw I could borrow. There's no easy way to say this. Your house looks trashed. I think you need to get over there."

"Did you see anyone? Touch anything? You didn't go inside, did you?" Joe grabbed his keys.

"I've watched enough cop shows to know I shouldn't do any of that," Andy said firmly. "I'm only sorry I didn't hear the assholes who did this."

Refusing to start worrying about what "this" was until he could see for himself, Joe thanked Andy and told him he'd be out there as quick as he could. Hanging up the phone, he debated for all of two seconds. Liam and the others could be gone for hours yet, depending on what they found. Doc was expecting him home any minute. *I'll just stop in for a quick minute and warn him I might be late, then head out there.*

Hurrying out of the mayor's office, he barely stopped to smile or nod at people saying hello, his mind wondering just how bad the damage to his little house was. Fortunately, no one was in Doc's waiting room and the treatment room door was open.

"Joe, you're a wee bit early, but I'm happy to lock the door if you're home for the evening." Doc's smile settled something deep inside Joe's heart and made his cock perk up, but he had to stay focused on getting out to his house.

"I'm really sorry but I have to go out and I don't know how long I will be," he said quickly. "Andy, my neighbor called. It could be a break-in, vandalism, I don't know, but it's my house. Someone's trashed my house."

"I'm coming with you," Doc said, standing and pulling off his white coat. "Come on, we can talk on the way."

"But…." Joe bit his lip just in time. Doc was his mate. Pregnant or not, the house was now theirs under shifter law and his mate was more than capable of looking after himself. He let out a long breath. "Thank you."

"Thank you, babe. I know that wasn't easy for you," Doc whispered as he stepped into Joe's personal space. "Remember, whatever it is, we can fix it."

Joe nodded mutely, following his mate out and around to the carpark. It seemed they were taking Doc's car and Joe really didn't mind because he wasn't sure he could drive safely. *I'm a professional. This is my job.* But the words brought him cold comfort. He couldn't dismiss the fact that someone, most likely a member of his family, was trying to kill him and it was most likely them who'd targeted where he lived.

The trip was silent, but Joe couldn't hold in his gasp of dismay as Doc pulled the car up in front of the place he'd called home for so long. The wooden exterior he'd lovingly sanded down and stained were covered in bright red painted words including "Die Traitor" and a number of graphic slurs used against gay men. None of the windows appeared broken, but the front door was hanging limply from one hinge.

"I'm going to shift and check around the outside," Doc said grimly, pulling his shirt over his head. "I can pick up scents better that way."

Joe nodded and got out of the car, his feeling of dread increasing as he climbed up the porch and peered through the smashed door. Scenting anything was impossible. The floor and walls were smeared with excrement. The stuffing from his couch spilled from jagged slashes in the covering and his television had a huge boot print in the middle of the shattered screen. Covering his nose with his arm, Joe stepped inside, quickly registering the smashed crockery on the kitchen floor and the mass of food that had been trampled into the hardwood.

There didn't appear to be anyone left inside but Joe kept a wary ear out for strange noises as he walked silently through the mess. Pushing open the door to his bedroom, Joe's heart almost stopped when he saw a man-sized lump on the ruined bed. Forgetting the stench, he hurried over, rolling the body so he could see the face. His Uncle Harold's blank eyes stared back at him. Joe didn't have to check his uncle's pulse to know he was too late. The huge hole in his uncle's forehead let him know it wasn't an accident.

"A funny thing happens to people when they betray their family, Joe. Did you know that?" A huge figure stepped out from the adjoining bathroom, pointing a rifle straight at him. The resemblance to the man on the bed was unmistakable.

"Uncle Myron, I didn't know you were in town." Joe backed away from the bed, his hands raised. *Stay outside, Doc, please stay outside.* "What are you doing here?"

"I think it's obvious, don't you?" Myron came closer, his frame back lit by the setting sun in the window beyond. "I'm here to restore honor to our family name."

Joe glanced at the dead body on the bed. "By killing them all?"

"Harold was a weak link – always had been." Myron sneered at the body. "Far too busy getting his dick shined to make a difference in this town and now I hear he was going to go blabbing to the council, telling family secrets. Robert had more of the right idea, but then you killed him, didn't you?"

"Only because he tried to kill me first." Joe tried to edge closer to the door, but a wave of Myron's rifle stopped him. "I still don't understand. You don't live in this town. You haven't done for years. Why do you care what happens here?"

"You've definitely got the smarts, boy, I'll give you that. Shame Al and Wall weren't similarly blessed, but then they took after their mother's side of the family."

Joe pressed his lips firmly shut, his eyes looking for a means to escape. He could shift, but a rifle of that size was going to do damage no matter what form he was in. He really didn't want Doc to have to pull bullets out of him again.

"Cat got your tongue?" Myron sneered. "Oh, I forgot, you didn't mate a cat, did you? No, word around town is you hooked up with the local doctor. Now, why would you want to go and do something like that? There's some nice ladies in this town. I've seen them."

When? Where? But Joe didn't ask those questions. Instead, he said, "I thought shifter towns were beneath you. You've always preferred living and running your business in human towns like Jackson. Wall and Al used to boast you've got contacts as far away as New York."

"You're right, boy, you're so right. Humans are so much more fun to play with. They can't scent a lie, they quake when anyone shows a flash of fur. It's ludicrous how quickly they bow to my commands."

"That wouldn't happen here." Joe thought fast. He needed to catch Myron off guard if he was going to get the gun away from him. "Why are you so hell bent on having the Quincy's rule this town again? Harold and Robert never did anything for you. They were too selfish, looking out for themselves."

"True. True. You make a lot of sense." Joe tensed as Myron reached inside his leather jacket and pulled out a cigar and a lighter. Holding the rifle loosely in one hand, he stuck the end of the cigar in his mouth and lit it before returning the lighter to his pocket.

"The thing you never understood, boy, is there's honor among the criminal element, even in thugs like me. Harold and Robert might have been weak, but they were useful contacts to have. Harold had access to unlimited funds and resources in his position as mayor and was never capable of saying no to me. Robert was useful in wiping clean any little issues me and my friends might have had with the law. He always demanded payment, but then he never knew I was getting the money from Harold in the first place. The only question you have to answer, is are you going to be as useful, or do I have to dispose of you too?"

"What happened to Hargraves?" Joe was playing for time. Hopefully Doc realized they weren't alone and had called for help. Myron seemed perfectly relaxed, puffing on his hand rolled cigar, but Joe wasn't stupid. That situation could change in the length of time it took to pull the trigger.

"Hargraves, Hargraves." Myron took another drag on his cigar. "Oh, you mean that human lawyer? Yes, well, I couldn't allow him to spill his guts to the shifter council, could I? That boy would do anything for a roll of quarters, but he had no luck at all when it came to picking winning horses. He's another useful contact to have when it comes to getting charges squashed with human law enforcement."

"He owes you, in other words. Why didn't you just kill him and leave him with the dead council guard, if he knew too much? Why bother going to the trouble of springing him out of jail before your men blew it up?"

Myron laughed, causing a plume of cigar smoke to erupt from his mouth. "Always loyal to your position, boy. Trying to get a confession out of me?"

"I don't need you to confess," Joe said with more confidence than he felt. His animal was angry and wanted out and he was worried sick about where Doc had gone. Every second the standoff continued, Doc was in danger. "Wall and Al spilled their guts to the sheriff and the council guard, blaming you for everything. Maybe you should have taken them out instead."

"Those ungrateful shits!" Myron threw his cigar on Joe's gleaming floor and stamped on it. "And people wonder why I have to go around killing my fucking family members. Doesn't anyone understand the rules about keeping their fat traps shut anymore?"

"They were saving their own useless hides," Joe spat back. "That's all anyone seems to care about in the Quincy herd. They want to do what they like, when they like, ruin lives for other people, cause havoc wherever they go and then they start crying for their momma the moment the law catches them. If you'd all had an ounce of decency and worked hard and kept on the right side of the law, none of this shit would have happened."

"Well, well, well. Look who's developed a backbone at last." Myron laughed. "Maybe mating the Doc was just what you needed to remove that stick from out of your ass."

"Don't you mention my mate's name." Joe's fingers curled into fists and his shoulder's shook. "My mate has got more decency in his whole body than you have in your trigger finger. That gun you're pointing at me just about sizes you up, doesn't it? You never want to get your hands messy, always sending in someone else to do your dirty work for you. You couldn't take me in a fair fight in either form. No. You stand there behind your gun and think it makes you a big man. That is not the shifter way." Joe laughed harshly. "But then when was the last time you let your animal run free. You think being a buffalo is beneath you, too."

"Now look here, boy." The finger on the rifle trigger tightened as Myron snarled. "I admire spunk the same as the next man, but you don't know anything about me so keep your big mouth shut."

"Or what? You're already planning to shoot me." Joe didn't know where his recklessness was coming from, but from the moment Myron mentioned Doc he realized he had to keep his mate safe, even if that meant his death. "I can imagine the crime scene now. Harold dead on my bed. Me dead on the floor, the rifle you're holding, left in my hand to implicate me. You've been hanging around humans too long. You must think shifters are stupid. Your scent is in this room. Your damn scent is probably on Harold's body. The new sheriff isn't a buffalo, he's an alpha wolf shifter. You think he's not going to know you were here?"

A flicker of uncertainty crossed Myron's face. Unfortunately, it didn't last. "I'll be long gone before they get here."

"And how do you propose to get out of here, Myron? Fly? You or your men might have smeared my house with someone else's shit, but your scent still lingers, and you will be found." Joe let his anger and worry fuel his strength. "You've not lived in this town for decades. I've been here my whole life. My neighbor, who called me out here because he saw the damage to my house, will have already told a dozen other people what's been going on. People care about me in this town – the one thing you've never thought to cultivate. Relationships, Myron. Decent, caring, loving relationships. And because those people care about me, they will track your ass down, no matter how long it takes."

As if to punctuate Joe's statement, they both heard the sounds of footsteps on the porch. "How many people are you going to kill to save your worthless ass, Myron?" *Please don't be Doc, Please.* "Are you going to kill the whole town just so you can get away?"

Joe took a step closer to Myron as they both heard a loud thump and the scrabble of claws on the outside wall. "Have you got people who care about you? Because I have. My mate will be first in line, hunting you down, but there are so many more of us – more than your mind could comprehend. Do you remember Mrs. Hooper from the store – the Texas Longhorn? Have you seen the size of her sons lately? They grew up into fine strong lads.

Did you know two of Trent's brothers work for the council guards now and they're in town?"

Myron gulped and a faint sheen of sweat appeared on his forehead.

"But that's not all we've got in town. You won't have met the newcomers. Someone might have told you our new Mayor is a tiger, but did they tell you how big he is in his shifted form? And he brought some wonderful friends with him when they moved into town. Simon the lawyer who shares his animal spirit with a big-assed snake, Brutus the bear. Oh, did you know the other Sheriff deputy is an alpha lion shifter? He and his twin brother both care about what happens to me. Are you seeing a trend here?"

Myron started backing up and he carefully rested the rifle against the bed. "Look, I've done nothing to any of these people," he said as he straightened up. "They've got no cause to come after me. Harold was banished from here. The town should be thanking me for killing him."

"But it wasn't him you were after, was it?" Joe caught a flicker of something moving in the bathroom and held his position. "You wanted to kill me. You trashed my house, you were the reason the sheriff's office is sharing the mayor's building. And why? Because of family loyalty? The Quincy's never had any loyalty to each other. You just got pissed off because I made something of myself and the rest of you didn't."

"Look, Joe," Myron spread his hands wide as he backed up a bit more. "I'm sure we can come to some agreement. I was a bit pissed off when the Quincy's were kicked out of town, I'll admit it. But I'll pay for your house. Damn it, I'll build you a whole brand new one, big enough for you and your mate to share. I'll even pay to have the sheriff's offices rebuilt – more modern and bigger than they ever were before. Just get me safe passage out of here. I'll do anything you want."

"I want you to stop moving."

"Stop moving? Why?"

"Because you're about to stand on my mate's tail."

"Your mate?" Myron turned. "Holy fuck, NO!"

Joe wasn't ashamed to say he looked away. Buffaloes were herbivores as a rule. And Doc had every reason to be upset. Leaving a dead guy on his bed was cock-block material. Besides, his mate was pregnant. He was probably hormonal. Joe leaned on the door frame, eyeing the ceiling while he waited for the screams and sounds of teeth crunching bones to die down.

"Everything okay in here?" Rocky stuck his head around the door. "Someone's made one hell of a mess of your house."

"Yeah. It's worse in here." Joe waved at Harold's body, trying not to look at the blood smeared on the door into the bathroom.

"That freaking mate of yours is amazing, man." Rocky surveyed the carnage with a bright smile on his face. "I do wish he'd let me deputize him."

"He'll be busy for a few months. He's pregnant."

"Wow, congratulations, dude." Rocky slapped Joe on the back hard enough to hurt. "Nice to know that monster between your legs actually works properly."

Joe's cheeks immediately heated. "It's not the sort of thing you're supposed to notice."

"Not notice?" Rocky rolled over with laughter. "Man, you can see what you've got hanging between your legs from space."

A low growl sounded from the corner of the room and all eyes moved in that direction. The Komodo dragon had a piece of gristle hanging from his bloodied jaws and his teeth were bared.

"Yeah, I saw nothing," Rocky said, shaking his head. "Nothing at all. Never seen your mate naked ever, Doc, and never will. Will avert my eyes if he ever shifts in front of me again and…."

"Shut up, Rocky," Mal said fondly coming into the room. "I do have one question, changing the subject completely. How did Doc get in through the bathroom window in his shifted form? I know that's how he got in because there're huge claw marks gouging the exterior wood paneling. But I thought Komodo's couldn't climb."

"I guess my mate didn't want to see me wearing bullets again." Rolling his shoulders, Joe relaxed and cricked his neck before opening his arms in the Komodo's direction. "Come here, babe. You've got stuff caught in your teeth and I doubt I've got enough dental floss to cope."

Joe didn't understand why Rocky and Mal thought that was funny. It was true. He was fresh out of dental floss.

Chapter Twenty One

Doc shivered and without saying a word, Joe pulled a throw rug from the back of the couch and wrapped it around his shoulders, before resting his arm on top of it which helped. In deference to Doc's need for food and a long hot shower, the debriefing was being held in Doc's apartment, after the bodies of Myron and Harold had been disposed of. Joe's house was still trashed, but Liam had fixed the front door enough to close the place up. A lot more relaxed now, Liam was sprawled out on a rug, licking the last of chicken wings from his fingers. Rocky was at the table gobbling down one of Mrs. Hooper's stews while Mal was foraging through the fridge looking for another one.

"I'm not sorry for what I did." Doc felt he should get that out of the way before anything else. "Myron was a menace and a murderer, and he was going to kill Joe. He deserved to die."

"You won't get any argument from me," Rocky waved his fork in Doc's direction. "I think a lot of people will sleep easier tonight knowing he's gone. Harold too, I would think, although it wasn't as though he was evil."

"No, just a groveling wind bag with delusions of grandeur." Doc was still on edge. Despite his open acceptance of the killing, Joe had barely said anything since they'd got home. Doc mentally scolded himself for being so tactless. "I'm sorry, babe, I know they were your family."

"I'll sleep easier tonight knowing they're both dead," Joe said calmly, "but that still begs the question, what to do about the younger Quincys?"

"Al and Wall will have to go before the council," Mal said, popping a bowl into the microwave. "Although they didn't bomb the sheriff's office themselves, they were still responsible for hiring the men who did do it. I'm guessing we can't go for restitution, given most of the Quincy assets were sold when they were banished. Is there anyone else you can think of who might start causing us problems, Joe?"

Doc watched his mate as Joe answered. The man's jaw was rigid. "No, I don't think so. Harold has two daughters who are both married and were long gone before anything happened here. There were other cousins – lots of others, but Myron was right in one respect. The Quincy name is now mud in Arrowtown and I doubt we'll see any of them around here again."

"Was Myron mated?" Liam asked as he pushed his box of chicken away. "Gods, these wings will make me fat. Thank goodness I have two mates who will help me work off some calories."

"I never heard of Myron having a mate, and I doubt it," Joe said slowly. "He never trusted anyone to get close enough to him to do that. Harold and

Robert both had mates, but from what I know about my aunts, I would say their mate's deaths will come as a relief. It's not as though any of my family were true mated."

"Does that mean we can put this Myron business behind us?" Liam asked hopefully. "Only in case you missed what I said, I do have two mates and a son that I haven't seen all day…."

"Get on home with you, you, horny beggar," Mal laughed. "I'm sure Doc and Joe don't need your pheromones stinking up the place. Keep your phone on you but take tomorrow off. That goes for you too, Joe. Rocky and I have to be on deck tomorrow as the council are sending construction workers to start working on the new offices. Hopefully, the most we'll have to contend with in terms of crime is Old Clifford letting his pigs out again or Mrs. Gentry complaining about something spooking her chickens."

"You don't have to tell me twice." Liam jumped up and after throwing his rubbish in the trash bin, was out the door. Doc heard his bike rumbling down the street as he sped for home.

"I'm guessing you two have a lot to talk about as well, Doc and Joe," Mal said, tapping Rocky on the shoulder. "Joe, you've done a lot of shifts lately, and I know you've got a lot to do with your house. By law you're entitled to a mandatory three days off to spend with your mate. Why don't you take them? In fact, take a week. Ra's approved the funding for an extra deputy hire, now you and Liam are both mated. It's not fair that you get all the night shifts now."

Joe nodded. "Whatever you say boss." After grumbling about how he was still hungry, Mal dragged Rocky off to Cam's and the house was silent.

Sliding his hand across Joe's stomach, Doc rested his head on his mate's broad shoulder. "We're alone now, babe. Why don't you tell me what's upsetting you?"

/~/~/~/~/

Joe's stomach cramped, his head hurt, and he felt as though his skin was ready to peel off his body. He knew Doc meant well and was only concerned for his welfare, but if he opened his mouth Joe was going to end up crying like a baby and Doc deserved better than that from him. He was going to be a father now, he needed to be a man.

"I'm not sure the house can be saved," he said controlling his emotions through sheer force of will. "It…it…." Damn it, he was going to cry, he just knew it. "It might be better if we just got a bulldozer in and started from scratch." There, he'd said it. Now if he could just get rid of the water in his eyes without it falling down his face….

"Babe." Doc shocked him by swinging around and sitting on his lap, cupping his face in his hands. "That house was your home, the first safe place you ever knew. We're not bulldozing it. I told you before, it can be fixed. We will fix it."

The words were there, right on the tip of his tongue. *It's just a house.* But Myron had known how to hurt him. Until Doc, that place had been his sanctuary and every plank in it carried his blood, sweat and tears. "We both work, full time," Joe said hoarsely, trying to be pragmatic. He could not meet Doc's eyes. "It would take a lot of work, more than we have time for. Most of the furniture is only fit to be burned and that's without all the fecal matter spread over everything else. I just...I don't...." Joe bit back anything else he had to say.

"Look at me, babe." Joe slowly raised his eyes. What he saw in Doc's made his heart flutter. He could see it – he could see the love Doc had for him, shining from his eyes. And then his eyes widened because damn it all, he thought he could hear the words inside his head. *I love you, Joe Farriday. You're not alone anymore and we will fix that lovely sanctuary of yours and make it ours. Do you hear me?*

"You're talking in my head." Joe's voice squeaked, and he quickly coughed before saying in a deeper voice. "That was you, wasn't it? I'm not dreaming again?"

"I wasn't sure it would work. But if you're wondering if the words I love you Joe Farriday were true, then yep, you heard me correctly. Can you feel me in your head?"

Joe wanted to close his eyes, but he didn't want to look silly. He could feel his buffalo rumbling gently under his skin, but there in his head, there was something else. Or more specifically someone else. He'd just never noticed it before because he'd never thought to feel for it. "No one in my family was ever true mated," he whispered.

"I didn't know it was possible." Thinking hard, he tried to tune into their connection. Once he knew it was there, it was easy.

I love you too, Nathan Farriday. I promise I will do all I can to be a good mate to you and the best possible father to our children.

Doc's breath caught, and then all of a sudden Joe's lips were being feasted on, and while he didn't like the thought, Joe was so glad Doc had cleaned his teeth – twice. His brain was a little slow to catch up. He was still mourning his house, but Doc's lips had a way of clearing his brain of anything and when he finally pulled away, Joe was struggling to breathe for all the right reasons.

"You need something to take your mind off things, tonight." Doc's eyes gleamed.

"I thought we were working on that." Joe couldn't straighten out his cock because Doc was sitting on his lap, but he was happy to move their loving to another room – he'd just be happy to get his pants undone so his cock had room to move.

"Oh, we will be doing that." Doc winked. "I'm going to love the hell out of your ass and then you're going to do the same to me. But first, I was wondering, do you think you'd like to learn to use my ultrasound machine?"

"Your...?" Joe's brain had immediately headed for sexier pastures where he and Doc were both naked. But then realization hit him, and he looked down at Doc's shirt covered stomach. "You mean we might be able to see the baby, babies, or whatever?"

"It's the whatever side of things that is bothering me," Doc said wryly, "but, the way I look at it, if we see what's going on in me, then we can work out how much time we can devote to fixing our house. Good idea?"

Holding Doc's hips to stop him getting up, Joe confessed quietly, "Myron really hurt me today, and it had nothing to do with that gun he was pointing at me. I've never been a hateful person but I'm not sorry he's dead."

"I understand, and that's why we're going to fix our house. You don't let the bastards of this world take away those things that are important to you. I wasn't sure why you were so quiet but after you offering to floss my dragon's teeth, I didn't think it had anything to do with the killing."

"I wanted to be strong, but ever since we got back here all I wanted to do was break down and cry." Joe shrugged as he bit his lip. "When it's all said and done it's just a house, I do know that. While Myron was holding the gun on me, all I could think about was your safety. You're the most important part of my life."

"But that house is a part of you too, babe, and I can see us making many lovely memories in that place which is why we're going to fix it. You watch. We might be loners, but we know a lot of people. It won't be as hard as you think it will be." Leaning forward, Doc brushed a sweet kiss on Joe's forehead. "As for shedding tears, you have every right to. Don't hide that side of you from me. That's what having a mate is all about – having someone to hold you when the world around you falls to pieces. Now come on, let's head downstairs and I can teach you a new skill. And anytime, anytime at all you need me to hold you, just let me know." Doc tapped his head. "No one else need know about it."

Joe just had to kiss Doc after such sweet sentiments from the normally standoffish man. Not for long though. It really was painful when a semi-erection was caught in the creases in his pants. Understanding, for whatever reason, Doc wanted to have the ultrasound now, he followed Doc downstairs and watched as he set up the equipment.

"I'm really not sure if this is going to work," Doc said as he peeled off his shirt and climbed onto the bed. He ran his finger over the leathery part of his torso. "Usually, when I am using the machine on someone else, I can run the head of the sensing wand over their skin until I find the right place. Then I can push a bit, so the images are clear."

"Will it damage the equipment if I run this over your skin?" Joe looked at the wand warily. It just looked like a metal tube with a bulb on the top of it to him. "I could use a stethoscope and see if I can hear where the baby is before using the wand. Then I could just press in that spot."

"Babies have a nasty habit of moving around, especially in the early stages," Doc said. He waved at the stethoscope sitting on the cabinet by the bed. "Definitely have a go. If you do pick up a second heartbeat at least that means, we'll be having babies and not eggs."

Joe thought if Doc was carrying their young in eggs, then those eggs would have heartbeats too, but he wasn't going to argue. Resting the ultrasound wand in the holder on the trolley, he picked up the stethoscope and fitted the ends in his ears. The other end tapped against his hand and he jumped. The sound was surprisingly loud.

Before listening to Doc's stomach, Joe rested the end of the stethoscope on his mate's chest. Doc's heartbeat was slow but easy to hear. Doc laid still, his breathing even, and after a minute, getting used to the rhythm, Joe moved the end of the scope to Doc's belly. He hesitated, having no idea of pregnancy anatomy. Deciding to work from the belly button outwards, Joe was immediately thwarted when he realized Doc didn't have a belly button. *Idiot. He hatched out of an egg. Just guess where one would be.*

Doc chuckled but said nothing as Joe methodically moved the scope from one patch to another. The gut was a surprisingly noisy part of the body, Joe realized, with all sorts of gurgling and rumbling going on. Clearly, Doc's digestive system worked, and Joe could hear the underlying thump of Doc's heart. But it wasn't long before Joe heard something else – lighter, quieter and more rapid than Doc's heartbeat. Leaving the scope where it was, he unhooked one end from his ear. "I hear something," he said, knowing he was grinning from ear to ear.

"One, or….?"

Now he knew what he was listening for, Joe moved more rapidly. He quickly found another one, on the opposite side of Doc's torso. Straightening up, he suddenly noticed a lighter patch on the gray of Doc's stomach. "Have you always had this?" Joe traced the circular patch with his fingernail.

Leaning up on his elbows, Doc scowled. "No, that's new." He stabbed the lighter area with his finger. "Doesn't hurt though and it doesn't look like it's flaking or anything. It might be a pregnancy mark. Some species do have them. Did you hear more than one?"

"Two, I think," Joe said. "They're on opposite sides of your body. Is that normal?"

"You know as much as I do about this," Doc said, lying back down again. "Let's see if we can find anything with the machine." He turned his head, so he could watch the screen.

Checking the sweet fast thumps with the stethoscope once more, Joe reached over and grabbed the wand, placing it where the scope had been. Glancing over at the screen, he saw nothing but static, but then he wasn't sure how an ultrasound worked.

"Press down a bit harder," Doc said. "Actually, use some lube on the end of it and then try again."

Now is not the time to be thinking about probing things and lube, Joe thought as he did as he was told. The static wavered a bit on the screen, but that was the only change.

"Damn Komodo quirks," Doc scowled. "Try here." He pointed to the middle of the lighter patch of gray skin. Still nothing. Doc sighed. "Thanks for trying, babe, but I think we're going to have to wing it with this pregnancy. Did you want another listen before I get up?"

Nodding quickly, Joe put the end of the stethoscope back in his ear. *There's one,* he thought as he put the end of the scope on one side of Doc's stomach, *and there's the other one.* To make sure he wasn't hearing just one, super loudly due to stomach acoustics – yep, he knew nothing about that either – he pressed the scope end in the middle of Doc's stomach too. The sounds were a lot fainter there, but his keen ears could pick up two distinct rhythms, one slightly faster than the other.

"Two distinct heartbeats," Joe grinned as he straightened up again. "Both of them are quieter and faster than yours, but one of them is running slightly quicker than the other."

Sitting up, Doc swung his legs over the side of the bed. "Let me listen," he said quietly, holding out his arm so Joe could come close. Hooking one of the ear buds out of Joe's ear, Doc put it in his own ear and with a hand each holding the end of the scope, Doc and Joe shared a long loving look as they listened to the two new signs of life Doc was carrying.

Chapter Twenty Two

The last thing Doc expected as he and Joe drove up to Joe's house, two days after he killed Myron, was to find the yard, the driveway and all the surrounding area covered in cars, trucks, and people. Dozens of people. Someone had set up a marque, there were a few children running around, someone was grilling steak and sausages, and somewhere in the bedlam a baby was letting his parent know it was time for a feed. Standing in the middle of the chaos Doc spotted Ra – one of the taller men in the area. Doc climbed out of the car and reached for Joe's hand. It seemed his precious mate was in shock.

"Doc, Deputy Joe, so glad you two finally crawled out of bed." Ra beamed as his arms swept the crowd. "We weren't sure what to do with all your personal bits and pieces, not that there was much left undamaged, I'm afraid. But what do you think?"

"What's happening?" Joe's eyes were wide. "Who...what...how?"

"We called a town meeting." Ra laughed. "Me and the guys were sitting around the night Myron was killed, chatting like we do. Mal mentioned you were upset over the damage to your house, and we were trying to think of ways to help. It was my precious Seth who suggested we hold a town meeting and see who could pitch in. We didn't want to disturb your mating celebrations, so we got stuck in and started doing what we could."

"The whole town must be here." Doc nodded at Forest who stalked past scowling with three long planks on his shoulder. "This is incredible."

"We do hope you don't mind." Seth came running over, his blond curls gleaming in the sunshine. "We talked about it and realized that town meetings didn't just have to be times when we come together to punish someone. They can be used for good too. Everyone here volunteered their time or goods, whatever we needed. It's a great community bonding exercise."

"I just can't believe it." Joe was blinking rapidly and seemed to be having trouble breathing. Doc moved closer, wrapping his arm around his mate's waist.

"You'd better believe it," Rocky yelled from the porch. "It's pretty much done. But get your ass in here. Mal's nagging me about color schemes and you know I know nothing about that shit."

Weaving their way through the crowds of people who all seemed to have something to do, Doc saw Dan unloading wood from the back of his truck – Jenny beaming as she supervised. Brian, Roe, and Carmine were giving the window sashes a fresh coat of paint, while Mrs. Dash was trying to keep Rosie out of the paint. Mrs. Hooper was there, yelling at her boys. "Don't think you're going to get out of working if you fall off that damn roof." Simon was flexing his muscles as he was hammering in some new cladding, being handed nails by a drooling Darwin. Cam had set up a bar on one side of the marque, handing out beers held in giant coolers filled with ice.

Inside was swarming with people. Doc remembered with a pang, the tears Joe had shed just two nights before. The most prevalent memory was the stench but now there was nothing but the slight smell of lemon bleach. Seth's mother Ella was supervising a group of female rabbit shifters in the kitchen who were restocking freshly painted cupboards with enough supplies for a month. Liam and Lucien were organizing a new book case with Gareth and Barney. From the boxes of books at their feet, it seemed Lucien had brought around half of his store. The lions' mates, Beau, Trent and Noah were arguing about the best placement for a plastic shrouded couch that looked big enough to sleep on. Even the carpet under their feet was brand new.

And in the middle of it all stood Mal complete with a clipboard. "Thank goodness you two are here. I swear I'm going to kill Rocky one of these days and no one will blame me. Look, I'm just going to say it straight. Rocky ordered the damn thing before I could stop him and now it's here and it's freaking huge and...oh shit. You might as well see for yourself." He turned and picked his way through the busy living room, heading for the bedroom.

"I told him," Mal continued as Doc kept Joe close to his side. "I said something like this should be a personal choice. You two should have picked it for yourself. But no, that man's got a heart of gold and he thinks with his dick. I am so sorry." He threw open the bedroom door and stepped back so Doc and Joe could go in.

"Wow." Doc could understand Joe's sentiment. The last time he'd seen the master bedroom the floor was covered in blood and there was a dead body on the bed. That bed, and the flooring had been replaced along with the doors and curtains. The tang of paint filled the air. But that wasn't the reason for Joe's wow.

Dominating the room was the biggest four poster bed Doc had ever seen and he'd been alive three centuries. But it wasn't the height of the bed that caught anyone's eye, nor the nets hanging from the railings around the top and for now tied back against the four wooden pillars. It was the carvings that adorned the headboard, the baseboard and scrolled their way up all four posts.

"This is Rocky's way of getting back at you for growling at him when you thought he'd noticed my dick," Joe clapped his hand over his mouth as he laughed. "Look at them. Look at the carvings. What's the main thing anyone looking at this would notice."

"Huge dicks." Doc shook his head as he chuckled. Because sure enough, every spare inch of wood was filled with males supporting appendages well beyond the laws of averages. And they weren't just holding those dicks either. There was a carved mass orgy on the woodwork, with cocks stuffed in asses and mouths, sometimes more than one at a time. "Rocky!"

"You yelled?" Rocky poked his head through the open window, eying Doc nervously.

"Are you trying to set us up on pornography charges if we keep this thing?"

"That's not pornography, that's artistic expression. I'll have you know it's a collector's item." Rocky stuck his nose in the air.

"You heard him, babe," Doc said to Joe. "In front of witnesses too. So Rocky, where did you get it?"

"Why? They won't take it back. It was a commission piece."

And probably cost a fortune, you daft, lovely man. Doc shook his head. "I don't want to return it, I want to get a matching set of dressers and bedside cabinets."

"Yeah?" Rocky's face broke out in his trademark grin. "I told you they would like it, Mal. I've already got the set," he winked. "I'm storing them in Ra's workshop away from the kids."

"Oh shoots, kids." Joe looked over from where he was pressing on the mattress. "Doc, we can't...."

"Yes, we can." Doc moved over to join him, pulling him into a kiss. "This is our sanctuary, remember. And Rocky's right. This is art. Once the kids are old enough to understand what they are seeing, they will be old enough to understand the concepts behind us having our own space. Besides, by that stage, they'll be watching porn on the internet and that is far worse than this. I think it's amazing and a very thoughtful gift."

"I knew you had a kinky streak, Doc." Rocky laughed. "I wasn't sure about my innocent deputy, but I knew there was more to you than starched white coats."

"I suggest you disappear, Rocky and you too Mal," Joe said with a sexy growl. "Or you'll realize just how much I've learned since Doc and I claimed each other."

/~/~/~/~/

The sun was just setting as Joe slipped away from the crowds enjoying a meal and the evening air. He needed a few minutes to himself. Barring a few minor details, the house was completely finished and there was nothing left to remind him of the horrible confrontation he'd faced just two days earlier. Rather than disappear home, the people of Arrowtown had stayed, enjoying a chance to socialize probably more so than they ever had before. The townspeople were always friendly with each other, with a few exceptions and tonight even Mrs. Hooper was being convinced to flick her skirts as she danced around the campfire.

The whole day had been an unreal experience. Joe had always loved the town he served, but he'd never really felt a part of it. And yet, all day, he was reminded with simple words and gestures that the town not only noticed him but cared about him too. There'd been one minor incident, when Lander, who'd been stealing beers from Cam's cooler had cornered him at the back of his house and tried to rub off on him. Joe hadn't even realized the boy was attracted to him. But a quiet snarl from Doc had the boy running back to his friends, and Joe liked to think by morning, Lander would have forgotten the whole incident. If he didn't, Joe was equally certain Hazel would see to it her boy didn't cause him any trouble.

"What you said to Myron was right you know, about this being a real caring community." Doc stepped out of the shadows and Joe went into his arms willingly. "These people care about us, no matter what we might have felt in the past. It's quite a humbling feeling, isn't it?"

"I always thought they didn't see me," Joe admitted as he freed Doc's hair from its leather tie and ran his fingers through the gray strands. "Now I wonder if they didn't know how to show me they did – that it was my fault because I was so aloof from them."

"You never had a reason to trust anybody," Doc said quietly. "I think this is a new start for both of us, don't you?"

"We've got babies coming," Joe lightly rubbed over Doc's covered abs. "You know we're going to be inundated with advice when that happens, don't you?"

"It's not a bad thing when people want to help." Joe noticed Doc's eyes were closing and realized his poor mate had been on his feet all day.

"How about we sneak off, go back to town. There's no one there. You can see how loud you can make me yell your name as I'm coming."

"Just one thing I need to know and call me hormonal or whatever you like but answer me honestly," Doc said gently. "Are you happy my sweet mate?"

"Yes." Joe was certain about that point. It wasn't because his horrible family members were dead and the threat hanging over his life was lifted, or even because of the wonderful way the good people of Arrowtown showed they cared for him and Doc. For the first time in his life he had someone who loved him unconditionally and who accepted his love in return. The two babies growing in Doc's belly were a welcome bonus he never dared dream of before. "I can honestly say, I couldn't be happier and it's all thanks to you."

Epilogue

Three months later.

"Your babies look beautiful, Jenny," Doc handed back the last triplet he'd checked over to a nervously waiting Dan. "Their weight is good, their skin is a lovely color and I see they all have your eyes, Dan. You've created a rabbit, a wolf and a hybrid mix. You must be very proud."

"Jenny's been amazing," Dan's pride was obvious. "Me, I just fell to pieces when she said she was in labor. How on earth are you going to cope?" He pointed to the really noticeable bulge under Doc's coat. "Are you going to be your own doctor?"

"I won't have much choice." Doc managed a smile as he slowly got up from his stool. The damn thing was just too low for him now and he was still getting used to his change in shape. "Fortunately, child birth is as natural as breathing and we've got months before Joe and I have to worry about that."

"You know, you're looking awfully big there, Doc," Jenny said nervously as she fussed over the two babies she held in her arms. "Are you sure your little one's aren't due to come already?"

"In theory, they shouldn't be, but you know mother nature. She can be sneaky sometimes." Doc was in a hurry to change the subject. "Now, don't worry about your little boy's cradle cap, that will clear up by itself, but if you have any concerns don't hesitate to bring them back in."

Fortunately, the sweet pair understood a dismissal when they heard one and within minutes Doc was alone again. It was nearly lunchtime and Joe was upstairs painting Doc's spare room. They were planning to turn it into a nursery. He should go upstairs and help, but in the past week everything, even going up and down the stairs, seemed to be so much of an effort.

"And I've got swollen ankles," Doc grumped as he looked down. Sure enough, he couldn't see his ankle bones. When his bump bloomed, and it did that faster than Doc thought possible, he'd taken to wearing shorts under his white coat and flat sneakers.

Checking to make sure the waiting room was empty, Doc closed the treatment room door and took out a pottle used for urine samples. He was well aware of the dangers of fluid retention. Deciding he needed to listen to the babies' heartbeats as well, just to double check everything was okay, Doc reached over for his stethoscope and that's when a massive sharp pain ran right across his stomach and he tumbled to the floor.

"Shit, shit, shit, shit." Doc fumbled with the buttons on his white coat as he screamed in his head for Joe. They didn't use their mind link very often, but he knew Joe would hear him. Sure enough, he heard pounding feet as Joe raced down the stairs.

"Babe, what's wrong?" Joe was surprisingly calm, coming over and picking Doc up from the floor and laying him on the new beds Doc had ordered just a month before. He spent so much time laying on it, seeing as he and Joe liked to listen to their little ones, Doc was determined to be comfortable. "Okay, that wasn't there this morning."

Doc looked down. Joe had undone the rest of his coat buttons and was gently prodding his stomach. The lighter patch of gray skin had grown over the past three months and now reached from his sternum to his pubic bone. Another wave of pain flew over his body as a gash appeared in the center of it.

"I'm giving birth," Doc panted, desperately reaching for Joe's hand.

"it can't be happening. You, me, our kinds have long pregnancies."

"Face it, babe, if you got much bigger these babies would split you right open. Can you lay back, on your side, or would you be more comfortable sitting up?"

"Sit, definitely sit." Doc had to watch what was going on. His mate was a law enforcement officer, not a medic. But Joe seemed surprisingly calm, gently prodding at the opening that looked like something Doc'd seen in a sci-fi movie. It was getting bigger and Doc's eyes almost fell out of his head as he saw what looked like a little hand coming out of the freaking opening.

"Shall I?" Doc looked up to see Joe watching him with patient eyes, his hands hovering expectantly over Doc's belly. A rush of pain rippled through his body again and his belly was almost split in two.

"Guess this isn't a good time to mention I am in no way ready for this," Doc gritted out. "Do it!"

With apparently endless calm, Joe slid his fingers carefully through the opening which was wide enough now to accommodate his whole hand. Doc had seen many a gruesome sight in his long life and performed more c-sections than he could count. But seeing Joe work calmly and quickly to bring a baby out of his stomach was surreal.

"Here we go," Joe said with a beaming smile. "One little girl with a full head of hair, and look, she has a sweet gray ankle bracelet. I guess she takes after you."

"Names. We haven't even thought of names." Doc's eyes filled with tears as he took the little precious while Joe returned his focus back to Doc's stomach. The child who'd spent his time resting on Doc's left side wasn't as keen to leave his warm home. Doc alternated between checking over the baby girl in his arms, while watching Joe gently coax the other one out of his belly. At least his pains had dulled down to a manageable ripple. That was one hell of a way to attract his attention and let him know the babies were ready to face the world.

"Here we go," Joe's gentle face shone with pride as the second child's foot finally slid free of Doc's belly. "A little boy, and with no noticeable gray skin marks...no, wait, this one has a circle of it on his back. Hmmm...." Joe bent and sniffed. "But he smells like buffalo." Leaning over he sniffed at their daughter too. "So, does she. It looks like we have two hybrids, babe. I'm so freaking proud of you. We're daddies. We're actually parents."

And that's when it hit Doc hard. These weren't two little ones he would pass on to their loving parents right after birth, like he'd done with Jenny and her triplets just two weeks before. He didn't have to watch them walk out of the door – well, not for another twenty years or so anyway. "These are ours," he whispered as tears rolled unchecked down his cheeks.

"Lie back, babe." Joe handed him their son and Doc realized getting the babies out was one thing, working out what to do with the hole he had up his middle was another. "I need to feel inside, I guess," Joe looked at his hands which were remarkably clean. "Shit, I didn't even wash my hands. What if you get an infection? What if I've done some damage in there? What if I've given germs to our babies?"

Joe's belated meltdown was sweet, but totally unnecessary. "We're shifters, babe, a bit of dirt isn't going to kill us or the little ones. Now," Doc struggled to think. "Get towels for the babies. We haven't got anything for them here. We'll have to put in a call to Mrs. Hooper and get some basics like nappies and formula."

Running to the cupboard, Joe got the towels while Doc continued thinking out loud. "We need a sign on the door. Cancel all non-urgent appointments for three days. Emergencies, well hopefully we won't get any of them. Work – you need to contact Rocky."

"I'm not leaving you stranded, Nathan." Joe seemed to have recovered some of his original calm. "What about your belly? You can't walk around like that."

Looking down, Doc saw that the gash wasn't as red or angry looking as it was before. He struggled to remember other species that went through something similar. Whales, he seemed to recall. Male whale shifters developed a slit for giving birth which closed naturally in about three days. Hopefully he would be similar. "Get some bandages, some of the wide ones from the cupboard under the sink. I'll get you to wrap me up and then we need to get these little ones some food." He looked down but both babies were sound asleep. They hadn't even cried, and Doc quickly checked to make sure their breathing was regular, which it was. *Some doctor I am,* he thought, angry at himself for forgetting the basic protocols for newborns.

Cut yourself some slack, Joe's voice sounded in his head and Doc jumped because he didn't realize he'd projected that. *You've done an amazing job and I love you, Nathan Farriday.*

I love you too. His cheeks heating, Doc held up the babies as best he could while Joe wrapped his torso in bandages. He'd just used the tape to hold it in place when there was a sharp knock on the treatment room door. "You decent?" Mrs. Hooper pushed open the door with the large basket she was carrying. "Now, I just knew it and it looks like I timed everything perfectly."

"Mrs. Hooper, what are you doing here?" Doc quickly checked to make sure his children's gray marks were hidden. "Is something wrong? As you can see, I have my hands full right now."

"You men are totally useless," Mrs. Hooper huffed as she handed the basket to Joe. "I asked this young 'un here what preparations you'd made for the babies and he said you both felt you had plenty of time and would deal with things later. Well, I thought to myself, I call bullshit because when I saw you waddling to the mayor's office that very same day I knew you were ready to pop. And just look at these sweet ones. Wrapped in towels. It's just as well I thought to make you up a basic care package."

"Doc, this is incredible," Joe said, peering through the basket. "Clothes, nappies, shifter-approved formula. Oh Mrs. Hooper you are a lifesaver. Honestly, I was going to call you just as soon as I'd put a sign on the door."

"Don't you go locking that door now. I've been on the phone all morning," Mrs. Hooper warned. "There's baby furniture coming and a whole stack more. Admittedly, none of it's brand new, but it's not as though babies do much damage. We pay it forward in this town, and all I ask is that when you're done with the basics, you pass them on."

"How have I never heard of this before?" Joe asked. Doc was too busy worrying what Mrs. Hooper would say when she realized the genetics his sweet ones carried. Would she be so keen to pay it forward then?

"Why would anyone talk to you about baby stuff?" Mrs. Hooper chuckled as she took in Joe's expression. "You've always been too busy keeping our teenagers in line. Now you're a dad, you'll learn about a whole new side of this town. Come on Doc, don't keep hogging your babies. I want to see."

With a sinking heart, Doc realized he had no choice. To refuse the town matriarch just wasn't possible especially when Mrs. Hooper had arrived like a baby angel bearing gifts. Ensuring his daughter was securely wrapped in a towel he handed her over. Coming to stand by his side, Joe took his hand, clearly sensing his discomfort.

"You are such a beauty," Mrs. Hooper cooed, so unlike her normal self, Doc almost fell out of bed. "A perfect blend of Komodo and Buffalo. You're going to break some hearts when you get older."

Komodo? Doc shared a worried look with his mate. "Mrs. Hooper," Doc said slowly, "how long have you known what animal I share my spirit with?"

Mrs. Hooper started laughing, her ample body shaking so hard the little girl's eyes flew open. "I've always known. Goodness. I don't know why you try so hard to hide it, but the old folks in the town can respect that you do. But now you've got little ones, you will have to rethink your decision. All Komodo dragon shifters are marked." She peeled back the towel from Doc's daughter's foot and grinned at the gray band of skin that looked like a ribbon around her ankle. "Your little one doesn't deserve to go through life feeling ashamed of this."

"It's not shame." Doc looked to Joe for comfort, feeling his eyes water as Joe bent down and held him close. "It's growing up never knowing where you truly came from. It's knowing how barbaric others view my kind. I didn't even know there were other shifters like me. There's nothing on the council website and I should know, I spent dozens of hours looking."

"Bah, the council are about as useful as a wet paper bag. You should talk to your elders. They know more about shifter lives than any website will tell you."

"Do many people know?" Doc didn't know what to think. He'd spent a lifetime hiding his lizard. He didn't understand why Mrs. Hooper didn't think it was a big deal.

"Most of the old people in this town, yes. The younger ones, maybe, maybe not. The thing is you and your mate, you've carved a permanent place in the heart of the people in this town. I thought you realized that when the town all pulled together and renovated the Deputy's house. Your children will be safe here – to be themselves, regardless of what form they shift into. That's the whole foundation of what a shifter town is. Don't you get it?"

Mrs. Hooper looked down at the newborn girl, who'd settled back to sleep. "More and more hybrids are being born all the time. I like to think our town is blessed, even more so now. Our mayor's children, that lawyer's Simon's children, Beau's – they are all hybrids. I saw Jenny with her wolf/rabbit hybrids just this morning when they came into the store. They are all gorgeous. They are all hybrids and I truly believe these children will show us how similar we are as shifters, instead of highlighting our differences. That's a real positive, don't you think?"

"You're right, Mrs. Hooper," Joe said quietly, taking his son into his arms. Doc's emotions were all over the place, but his arms immediately felt empty, which Mrs. Hooper seemed to realize too. Was there anything that woman didn't know?

"Make up at least eight bottles and store some in the refrigerator," Mrs. Hooper warned as she placed Doc's daughter in his arms. "You do not want to be fiddling with making up formula at two o'clock in the morning when these two are screaming loud enough to rock the foundations. Congratulations, both of you," she added as she bustled out the door as suddenly as she arrived.

"Wow." Joe shook his head, but as he was looking at his son at the time, Doc wasn't sure what the wow pertained to. He looked down at his daughter. Her blond hair, cute button nose and full lips. He could see features of both of them in her adorable face. He rubbed his thumb over her fragile ankle. The leathery skin was still soft and likely would be for some years.

"Hey," Joe's weight settled on the bed beside him. "Are you feeling okay? Do you need to sleep? Eat? Have a shower? What do you need?"

"I need a kiss, Deputy Joe Farriday," Doc smiled through his tears. "A good long kiss, because I have a feeling it will be the last one we have for a while."

"Are you happy?" Joe asked as he leaned forward, reminding Doc of when he asked that very same question of his mate.

"I can honestly say I have never been happier," he said, remembering what Joe's response was three months ago. "And it's all because of you, and them," Doc added fondly. "We've really got to think of some names."

Joe was still chuckling as he covered Doc's lips with his own.

The End.

Of course, it's not the end – there are countless more stories to come from Arrowtown and besides, we still need to find out what Doc and Joe's babies names are. They wouldn't tell me when I wrote this story. This book does hit a milestone for me though, which makes it doubly special in my eyes – this is my 50th MM (or MMM) title and I am so proud. Of course, with my to-do list a mile long, I don't have time to sit back and bask. There will be more books coming soon in the God's series where Thor meets someone unexpected for him and the

City Dragon series where Samuel has some unusual problems with his mate and that is just the next two on a very long list.

It seems strange to think back now, when I was writing my very first shifter book, (The Reluctant Wolf) that I didn't know any of you and none of you knew about me. I have to say it's been one hell of a journey and along the way I have made multitudes of good friends through social media. Just recently, you were there to cheer for me when I sold my house and cried alongside me when I lost my precious Scout and Scruffy. You inspire me with your pictures, your comments and ideas – honestly, I wouldn't have made it this far without you all. So, thank you for that.

As you will have seen on various posts on social media, authors are being plagued with people pirating their books. I am one of those authors and my income has suffered because of it. I hesitate to ask for reviews, because you all give me so much already, but reviews genuinely help new readers take a chance on a new author to them, so if you would like to say a few words wherever you purchased this book, thank you.

Remember, I love to hear from you all – email, PM on FB, or MeWe, or feel free to post in my special groups. All my contact details are provided on the last page of this book.

Thank you for being with me on this glorious journey.

Hug the one you love.

Lisa xx

About the Author

Lisa Oliver had been writing non-fiction books for years when visions of half dressed, buff men started invading her dreams. Unable to resist the lure of her stories, Lisa decided to switch to fiction books, and now stories about her men clamor to get out from under her fingertips.

When Lisa is not writing, she is usually reading with a cup of tea always at hand. Her grown children and grandchildren sometimes try and pry her away from the computer and have found that the best way to do it is to promise her chocolate. Lisa will do anything for chocolate.

Lisa loves to hear from her readers and other writers (I really do, lol). You can catch up with her on any of the social media links below.

Facebook – http://www.facebook.com/lisaoliverauthor

Official Author page – https://www.facebook.com/LisaOliverManloveAuthor/

My new private teaser group - https://www.facebook.com/groups/540361549650663/

And I am now on MeWe – you can find my group at http://mewe.com/join/lisa_olivers_paranormal_pack

My blog - (http://www.supernaturalsmut.com)

Twitter – http://www.twitter.com/wisecrone333

Email me directly at yoursintuitively@gmail.com.

Other Books By Lisa/Lee Oliver

Please note, I have now marked the books that contain mpreg for those of you who don't like to read those type of stories. Hope that helps ☺

Cloverleah Pack

Book 1 – The Reluctant Wolf – Kane and Shawn

Book 2 – The Runaway Cat – Griff and Diablo

Book 3 – When No Doesn't Cut It – Damien and Scott

Book 3.5 – Never Go Back – Scott and Damien's Trip and a free story about Malacai and Elijah

Book 4 – Calming the Enforcer – Troy and Anton

Book 5 – Getting Close to the Omega – Dean and Matthew

Book 6 – Fae for All – Jax, Aelfric and Fafnir (M/M/M)

Book 7 – Watching Out for Fangs –Josh and Vadim

Book 8 – Tangling with Bears – Tobias, Luke and Kurt (M/M/M)

Book 9 – Angel in Black Leather – Adair and Vassago

Book 9.5 – Scenes from Cloverleah – four short stories featuring the men we've come to love

Book 10 – On The Brink – Teilo, Raff and Nereus (M/M/M)

Book 11 – Don't Tempt Fate – Marius and Cathair

Book 12 – My Treasure to Keep – Thomas and Ivan

The Gods Made Me Do It (Cloverleah spin off series)

Book One - Get Over It – Madison and Sebastian's story

Book Two - You've Got to be Kidding – Poseidon and Claude (mpreg)

Book Three – Don't Fight It – Lasse and Jason

(The next book in this series will be about Thor)

The Necromancer's Smile (This is a trilogy series under the name The Necromancer's Smile where the main couple, Dakar and Sy are the focus of all three books – these cannot be read as standalone).

Book One – Dakar and Sy – The Meeting

Book Two – Dakar and Sy – Family affairs

Book Three – Dakar and Sy – Taking Care of business – (coming soon).

Bound and Bonded Series

Book One – Don't Touch – Levi and Steel

Book Two – Topping the Dom – Pearson and Dante

Book Three – Total Submission – Kyle and Teric

Book Four – Fighting Fangs – Ace and Devin

Book Five – No Mate of Mine – Roger and Cam

Book Six – Undesirable Mate – Phillip and Kellen

Stockton Wolves Series

Book One – Get off My Case – Shane and Dimitri

Book Two – Copping a Lot of Sin – Ben, Sin and Gabriel (M/M/M)

Book Three – Mace's Awakening – Mace and Roan

Book Four – Don't Bite – Trent and Alexi

Book Five – Tell Me the Truth – Captain Reynolds and Nico (mpreg)

This series is now finished, but I have promised a couple of short stories about the characters in book 5 so watch for those.

Alpha and Omega Series

Book One – The Biker's Omega – Marly and Trent

Book Two – Dance Around the Cop – Zander and Terry

Book 2.5 – Change of Plans - Q and Sully

Book Three – The Artist and His Alpha – Caden and Sean

Book Four – Harder in Heels – Ronan and Asaph

Book 4.5 – A Touch of Spring – Bronson and Harley

Book Five – If You Can't Stand The Heat – Wyatt and Stone (Previously published in an anthology)

Book Six – Fagin's Folly – Fagin and Cooper

There will be more A&O books – I have had one teasing my brain for months, so stay tuned for that one.

Balance – Angels and Demons

The Viper's Heart – Raziel and Botis

Passion Punched King – Anael and Zagan

(Uriel and Haures's story will be coming soon)

Arrowtown

A Tiger's Tale – Ra and Seth (mpreg)

Snake Snack – Simon and Darwin (mpreg)

Liam's Lament – Liam Beau and Trent (MMM) (Mpreg)

Doc's Deputy – Deputy Joe and Doc (Mpreg)

NEW Series – City Dragons

Dragon's Heat – Dirk and Jon

Dragon's Fire – Samuel and...wait and see ☺ (coming soon)

Also under the penname Lee Oliver

Northern States Pack Series

Book One – Ranger's End Game – Ranger and Aiden

Book Two – Cam's Promise – Cam and Levi

Book Three – Under Sean's Protection – Sean and Kyle – (Coming soon)

Standalone:

The Power of the Bite – Dax and Zane

One Wrong Step – Robert and Syron

A number of readers have asked me if Balthazar will get his own story. I am not ruling it out, but that is likely to be a short story rather than turn this into a full series.

Uncaged – Carlin and Lucas (Shifter's Uprising in conjunction with Thomas Oliver)

37324345R00235

Printed in Poland
by Amazon Fulfillment
Poland Sp. z o.o., Wrocław